Endlessly YOURS

CARRIE ANN RYAN

NEW YORK TIMES BESTSELLING AUTHOR

ENDLESSLY YOURS

SPECIAL EDITION

THE WILDER BROTHERS
BOOK TEN

CARRIE ANN RYAN

ENDLESSLY YOURS

Endlessly Yours
A Wilder Brothers Novel
By: Carrie Ann Ryan
© 2025 Carrie Ann Ryan

Cover Art by Sweet N Spicy Designs

For my Dad.

Thank you for sitting with me and answering so many questions for me when I wanted to know about the adjustment after getting out of the military.

Thank you for your service.

And for going along with it when I call the Wilder Brothers "our" series.

Thank you to all veterans for what you do. I know it isn't easy finding a new path when you become a civilian, but know you're not alone.

Especially right now when those you trusted are betraying you.

PRAISE FOR CARRIE ANN RYAN

"Count on Carrie Ann Ryan for emotional, sexy, character driven stories that capture your heart!" – Carly Phillips, NY Times bestselling author

"Carrie Ann Ryan's romances are my newest addiction! The emotion in her books captures me from the very beginning. The hope and healing hold me close until the end. These love stories will simply sweep you away." ~ NYT Bestselling Author Deveny Perry

"Carrie Ann Ryan writes the perfect balance of sweet and heat ensuring every story feeds the soul." - Audrey Carlan, #1 New York Times Bestselling Author

"Carrie Ann Ryan never fails to draw readers in with passion, raw sensuality, and characters that pop off the page. Any book by Carrie Ann is an absolute treat." – New York Times Bestselling Author J. Kenner

"Carrie Ann Ryan knows how to pull your heartstrings and make your pulse pound! Her wonderful Redwood Pack series will draw you in and keep you reading long into the night. I can't wait to see what comes next with the new generation, the Talons. Keep them coming, Carrie Ann!" –Lara Adrian, New York Times bestselling author of CRAVE THE NIGHT

PROLOGUE
BROOKS

BEFORE.

"**B**rooks, sit down with me."

"I can't," I said as I leaned forward and brushed at the little amount of peach fuzz on the top of her head.

Amara smiled up at me, that smile just as beautiful as the first time I had seen her all those years ago. We had been sixteen, the both of us waiting at the DMV for our driver's licenses. We might have gone to the same high school, but it wasn't as if I had known every single person on our campus.

And so, while waiting next to the girl with gorgeous blue eyes, blonde hair, and a retainer that she kept playing with, I knew that I was in love.

I just hadn't realized it was a love that was unending and broken until it was nearly too late.

"You should sit."

"I need to go get you some water. I'll be right back."

I didn't know why this panic kept gripping my chest. It wasn't as if this was a new feeling. A new state.

My beautiful wife, the woman that I had loved for over a decade, was dying in front of my eyes and I could not stop it. I used my hands to build things for a living. I constructed things. I made them sturdy. My goal in life was to make sure that what I built could withstand the test of time.

And yet, I could not keep my wife safe. She was fading before my eyes, and I could not just sit here and watch it happen. I needed to be doing something.

But there was nothing I could do.

"I have water. Come and sit down. We need to finish our show. And I want to ask you something."

And because I honestly could never say no to Amara, I sat down next to her, my hip against hers as I held her hand and ran my finger along her jaw.

"Let me get you your scarf. Your head must be getting cold."

She continued to smile up at me, and I did not like the look in her eyes. The resignation. The knowing.

Stage IV breast cancer wasn't always a death

sentence. That's what they kept telling me. But her cancer was aggressive and had spread to multiple areas of her body. That's what Stage IV was, after all. She had done multiple rounds of chemo and had lost her hair more than once. Now it was growing back because she was on radiation. The radiation that left burns along her body around her ports. The allergy she had developed to the adhesive having ripped off chunks of skin that were now being burned by the same medicine that was supposed to keep her alive.

I had no idea how Amara could do this. How she could keep so strong in the face of what was to come.

I was weak. Breaking inside, and yet my wife could withstand anything. That's what she kept telling me.

My wife smiled at me, the dark circles under her eyes deepening. "Before we start the show, I want to ask you something."

Again, I couldn't say no to her. I never could before. And sure as hell not now. "What is it, Baby? What can I do for you?"

"You always ask that. And you always say anything. But I'm going to ask something very scary. Can you do that for me?"

I froze, the lump in my throat making it difficult to breathe. "What is it? I'll do it. Anything you want." As long as it kept her here with me, I would do anything.

"I really need you to think about this. I need you to promise me that you'll think about what I'm saying and then promise me you'll do it."

"Just tell me, Amara. I promise, I'll do whatever you say."

"Don't regret those words." She squeezed my hand, and the energy sparked back into her eyes, the energy that I had been missing all these years.

Clawing panic squeezed my throat, but I tried not to let it show. I needed to be the strong one, because Amara was allowed to break down. She didn't at the hospital, didn't in front of her friends, but she was allowed to in front of me.

So I had to be the strong one.

"When I'm gone—"

"No," I cut her off. "No, we're not going to say those words."

"Brooks. I love you with all of my heart. But you know that it's not going to be much longer."

Another crevice opened up in my heart and I raged against whatever god would listen. "Amara. I'm going to yell. And you know I don't yell at you." My voice cracked, but she ran her fingers over my hand in answer.

"When I'm gone, I want you to clean out this house. Don't look at the boxes of bandages and scarves. Don't look at the house that has become my comfort and your horror."

"Amara."

I wasn't sure what I was supposed to say, though, and she squeezed my hand even harder. But there wasn't enough strength in that hand. Everything was breaking inside me, and I hated myself. It should be me in that bed. It should be me wasting away, but it wasn't. It was the sweetest girl I had ever met instead.

"I need you to promise me that you'll try."

"Amara," I said again, this time the tears freely flowing.

"Find love again. It's not fair. *Life isn't fair.* I don't know what's coming next, and I am being so mean to you right now. But I need you to move on."

"Don't you make me promise that. I'm not going to. You can't fucking ask me to do that." Every ounce of rage at her cancer coursed through me in that moment, and I couldn't catch my breath.

"But I can. It's the cancer prerogative." She smiled, but I couldn't reciprocate. That had been our running joke between us. Because when she needed ice cream or needed me to do something that I really didn't want to do, we mentioned the cancer prerogative. It was ridiculous, but sometimes we needed to find the humor in the hell. There would be nothing left if we didn't.

"No. Not this time."

"Brooks. My love. My best friend. Please. Try. Go out on dates. Find another woman. We both know that it's just been the two of us."

I swallowed that lump in my throat, nodding. We had both been sixteen-year-old virgins when we had gotten together, meaning the two of us had only slept with each other. And in my mind, that was how it was going to be. My one and only.

"You can't ask this of me."

Amara wasn't crying, but I was. I wasn't sure if she'd practiced this speech, or she was so dehydrated she couldn't cry anymore. "But I can. Don't die with me, Brooks. I need you to find that happy ever after."

"You're my happy ever after, Amara. That's what we promised."

"And I'm going to break that promise. I'm going to love you for the rest of my life. And I hate that I know it's not long enough. Love me, Brooks. Love me for all your years. But I also need you to do something else. Live. Find someone that loves you just as much as I do."

"That's not going to happen."

"It might. Your heart is so big, Brooks. You take care of your brothers. You take care of me. You have so much in you. Let someone take care of you for once. Don't give up on life because life is giving up on me."

Damn this woman. She'd always been good with words when I got lost in my head. And now every word cut like a knife.

"I hate you right now," I growled.

"No you don't." Her smile softened, her shoulders relaxing.

I leaned over and brushed my knuckle along her too thin cheek. "You're right. Because I could never hate you. But I love you so much. You can't make me promise that."

"But I'm going to make you anyway."

Tears streamed down my cheeks, and I leaned forward, pressing my lips to her chapped ones. "I promise," I lied.

And then I laid down next to my wife, and held her as we watched a movie, and I tried not to think of that promise.

Amara died three weeks later. And as I stood in my backyard, her ashes on the mantle inside, I swore that while I loved my wife, and would always do so, I was going to break our final promise.

Because I would never love anyone like I loved my wife. I didn't have it in me.

ONE YEAR LATER.

I was drunk. The amount of whiskey in my system was probably an issue. But I needed all of the alcohol. Every ounce in this bar if I had to. I couldn't be at home for this, and I didn't want to. I had already ignored the countless phone calls. The sad looks from our neighbors.

We all knew what today was.

I lost my wife one year ago today, and drinking wasn't going to bring her back.

But maybe I could pretend for this moment.

I was at an airport hotel bar of all places, having driven hours just to get out of my neighborhood, get out of the places that reminded me of the woman that I loved.

Somehow I had ended up near a major airport, and figured I would get on a plane and go somewhere. I didn't know where. I had a bag, and I'd fly somewhere. Do something spontaneous and uncaring. Anything that wasn't Brooks Wilder. For now, I would spend the night in this airport bar and think of something to do next. And get drunk.

"Another," I said into the din, and the bartender nodded, filling up my glass. Someone sat next to me, but I didn't bother to look over. The place was busy, people milling about, waiting for the hours to pass before they could go to sleep, and then hitch a ride onto the shuttle.

I knew that I wasn't making any sense. I was just going wherever the wind blew me. Only I didn't want to stand still. Because standing still would mean I would have to think of Amara.

"A glass of rosé please," a soft voice said from beside me, and I saw a woman out of the corner of my eye lower her shoulders in a deep sigh.

The bartender shook his head. "Sorry, we don't have any of that. White or red."

"Then how about whatever he's having," she said, using her thumb to point toward me.

The bartender immediately poured her two fingers of whiskey, and she nodded, before tilting her glass toward mine.

"Cheers."

I didn't feel like adding to that, but before I could say so or move my glass, she knocked back the entire glass in one sip and didn't even shudder.

Well, damn.

"Another please," she said, and the bartender gave us a look, before shrugging and pouring us some more. "You really don't have good taste in whiskey, but thanks," the woman muttered next to me, and I didn't really know why she was talking to me, but I continued to drink.

And again.

And again.

NOW.

I sat on a wooden bench that I had built with my own hands, staring off into the land that my family now owned. I was born a Wilder, but now I was a Wilder with my brothers and cousins, building something that meant something.

The sun was starting to set, and it was about damn time since it was nearly nine o'clock. I never really realized how close to the equator South Texas was. Well, it wasn't that close, but far closer than up north.

Someone sat next to me on the bench, breaking me out of my geography reverie, and by the vanilla scent hitting my nose, I knew exactly who it was.

"I don't really want to talk," I growled, annoyed with myself for speaking first.

"I know you don't." Rory didn't say anything else, and the two of us stared off into the distance, the sun taking its damn time to set beyond the horizon.

"Why are you here?" I asked, not speaking of this bench. But this town, this retreat.

"Because I have nowhere else to go."

And with that kind of answer, I didn't have much to say, so I sat next to the first woman that I had slept with after my wife had died, and didn't say a damn word.

And I swore I could hear Amara whisper in the wind, *"Try. For me."*

And I cursed under my breath and ignored that vanilla scent.

I had been drunk and had slept with someone who wasn't my wife. It didn't matter that Amara had been gone.

I'd broken something inside, broken everything.

And I still wouldn't keep my promise.

CHAPTER ONE
BROOKS

The thing about living alone for so long was that you sometimes got tired of waking up with a hard dick and having nothing else to do with it other than introduce it to your opposite palm for the morning so you didn't get bored with the other. With a sigh, I leaned against the shower wall, hot water spilling down my back, as I wrapped my left hand around the base of my cock and tugged. I licked my lips, imagining a faceless woman on her knees, her lips wrapped around the tip of my dick, careful of the piercings, with her tongue sliding in the slit at the tip.

I grunted, running my hand up and down my length, imagining the woman doing the same thing with her smaller hands. She would bob her head, her tongue flattening as she would let me slide down that pretty little throat. I'd pump in and out of those plump lips, loving the way that one hand would be squeezing the base of my cock, the other holding my thigh. Her nails would dig in, just at the point where pleasure turned to pain, and I would wrap her hair around my fist and slide deeper down her throat. Then I'd hold her still, eyes wide as I fucked her face, her hand moving down between her legs so she could get herself off, loving the way that she would take my cock.

Now my hand moved faster, imagining the way that my hips would move, and she would rock her body along with me. Only in my head, the hair around my fist turned blonde, and familiar gray eyes stared up at me. I cursed, but I didn't stop. Instead, I squeezed even harder, imagining the way that she would lap up every drop of me. I couldn't help but think about the way that her cunt would squeeze my dick once I slid into her from behind. She'd arch her back for me, and I would lick up every single tattoo that I knew dotted her spine. Then I'd bite down over the rose on her shoulder, and slam home, filling her with my cum, as she clamped down around my cock, coming right along with me.

I opened my eyes, sighing at myself as I moved the head of the shower to wash my cum off the shower wall.

"You're a sick, sick man, Brooks."

I knew I needed to stop having dreams about Rory. She wasn't mine. I knew that. She knew that. And we'd made our deals. Only I could practically smell her soft vanilla scent in my fucking bathroom. It had to be her lotion or something. I didn't want to think about it because I wasn't going to touch Rory in any way possible. I regretted every single moment we'd shared that night, and I wasn't about to lean into that desire or attraction once again.

I was Pavlov's dog, and she was the bell of my memories. Because as soon as she came around, my dick went to attention, and it took all within me not to figure out what the hell I was supposed to do with it.

As it was, Rory was spending way too many hours on the property. And I couldn't get her out of my mind.

I didn't want her. I wasn't sure I even liked her. And I didn't know her.

But my dick didn't answer to me. Nor did it ever listen to me. I did what it wanted. I quickly finished showering, paying extra attention to the Jacob's ladder piercing I had on my dick. It had hurt like hell when I had first gotten it, but that had been years ago, and it had healed up nicely. All I had to do was make sure when I got myself off, I didn't twist in a certain way. The women that I had been with since that fateful night in an airport bar where I'd had too much to drink, and too much grief to realize what a mistake I was making, had liked the piercing. Yes, they were a little afraid of it at first, especially if they wanted to wrap their mouth around it, but they got used to it. And with the condoms, the specialty condoms that I used, they could still feel it when it hit that spot, and in the end, they begged for more.

But I never gave it to them.

I had always been a one-woman man. From high school on, I had loved one woman.

And Amara was gone. My wife, my soulmate, was dead.

And now I never stayed with the same woman for more than a night. Was that breaking the promise that I hadn't truly made to her? I didn't think so. I was already going to hell for multiple reasons. By desecrating her memory by sleeping with a stranger that turned out not to be so unknown to me on the first anniversary of losing Amara, I'd taken the first of many steps in that direction.

What kind of hypocrite did that make me? What kind of hellscape did I deserve? Now, I slept with women that I met in bars, ones that I knew wanted nothing but a single night of pleasure, and we'd walk away without exchanging anything but a name.

And a few orgasms.

And yet with all those women over the years, it was Rory who continued to fill my daydreams when I needed to get off.

Rory—my brother's wife's best friend.

Of all the people in all of the world, it had to be her.

Honestly, the statistics didn't make any sense. I had met Rory miles away from here. Hell, I hadn't even lived outside of San Antonio at the time. My brothers and I had only moved here a couple of years ago when we had joined our cousins on this Wilder Retreat and Winery adventure.

I was a contractor and used my hands to build things for a living. So when my cousins had needed help in restructuring and adding on, I jumped at the chance to use my company for that. Because I was tired of sitting in a home that I used to share with my wife and pretending that I wasn't dead inside.

There had been too many dark nights where I had wanted to follow her, and that told me I needed to get a grip.

Amara would never forgive me for so many things but leaning into one thought that had been one dark thought too far, would have broken her.

So I'd moved outside San Antonio to the Wilder Retreat and Winery, along with my brothers.

Now we were one big happy family, the ten of us.

And every other person was married, with most of them either already having kids or talking about them.

I was the single man out, and I didn't care. It wasn't as if I was going to follow along with them. After all, I had been the first one to get married. I paused in my thinking. No, my cousin Evan and his wife Kendall had been married before me. They had been young, married too quickly, gone through hell, and after their divorce, had caught up again and gotten married. Their second chance was something that only made sense to them, but at least they were able to have one.

I was never going to have a second chance with Amara. Because cancer sucked, and it took everything from you.

I stopped pulling on my Henley and frowned. Why the hell was I focusing on Amara this morning? We had a family meeting, I had a shit ton of things to do at work, and I needed to avoid Rory because she kept coming onto the property to work with Ava. That meant I didn't have time to focus on the grief that seemed unending. It had been enough time that I should be okay. Or at least, should be able to go through the days without feeling like hell. And honestly, that was the truth. I could have an entire day where I didn't think about Amara, only to wake up in a desperate grip of grief.

Because I wasn't the man that Amara had married. Nor was I the man that had held her as she took her last breath.

I wasn't even the shell of a man who'd slowly meandered his way through the first two years without her.

I was Brooks Wilder. Contractor. Builder.

And grumpy asshole. I should probably put that last part on my business card. Just to warn people.

I looked in the mirror, realizing it was summer in Texas and 103 degrees today, and pulled off my Henley to find a T-shirt. Sometimes I forgot that I didn't live in the North anymore. Amara and I had lived up in Wisconsin for a few years, and that had been ingrained in me enough that I'd forgotten my Texas roots for a moment when I'd been on autopilot.

I shoved my feet into my work boots, tied them up, grabbed my wallet, keys, and phone, and hoped to hell that somebody made coffee at the retreat.

When my cousins had first opened *Wilder Brothers*, the Wilder Retreat and Winery, they'd just gotten out of the military and had needed to figure out what they were going to do with their lives. That side of the family had all joined up to the Air Force, other than our cousin Eliza, who'd married into the military instead with her first husband. My brothers and I hadn't joined the service but had gone our own ways. So when the cousins needed a way to blend back into society and figure out what to do with the rest of their lives, they bought this land with the winery and inn that had already been established.

Over the years they'd added to it, and I had helped along the way. Now it was one of the top ten inns and wineries in the state of Texas. Which, considering the size of Texas, was a big thing.

We had grown exponentially in the past few years, to the point that we had waitlists, celebrity weddings, and high-stakes security that my brother helped run.

All in all, I was glad that I didn't have to deal with a lot of the business aspects of it.

The cousins had all originally lived on the property as well. Now most of them had moved on with their families and moved out with their families, but each living close enough that they could be at the retreat in an emergency quickly. Some of them still lived on the land itself because there was enough acreage for that to happen.

In fact, my brothers and I had bought into the family estate by buying the land next to the original inn.

So now we have double the acreage and could expand.

My brothers still lived on property with their wives and families.

But I didn't.

I was a builder, it's what I liked doing.

So I'd built my home and a few other homes on another section of property that wasn't attached to the retreat.

Not that I wanted to be alone, which could always be an issue, but mostly because I wanted space and for my business not to be completely wrapped up in the other Wilder businesses. It was always good to have your finger in a number of pots. Everyone else did in the family.

So I had built my home and a few others on the property, so it was nearly a neighborhood, but it wasn't as if we were an HOA community with a groundskeeper or anything. I owned all of the homes and rented them out, and somehow, I created a fiefdom.

At least that's what my brother called it.

I shook my head and drove the few miles to the retreat.

I went in through the employee entrance, a new section that we had added in the past year, and nodded at the security who let me through. It was odd to think that this was our lives now, but I didn't mind it. I wasn't the complete loner and asshole that I'd been when I had first moved here, and I tried to be calmer and nicer.

But there was always an edge of anxiety these days.

And then as I parked my truck next to a familiar SUV, I realized exactly where that anxiety came from.

Of course Rory was here.

She wasn't going to be at the family meeting, but she was going to be on the property. Doing something. Probably drawing in one of the forested areas or near one of the creeks on the property. I didn't know precisely what she did, but she was here often enough that I couldn't escape her.

Lucky me.

Another truck pulled in beside me, and I lifted my chin at Wyatt.

"I guess we're both running late," my brother said as he jogged next to me so we could head in to the main area of the estate.

The property itself held a spa, over a dozen little cabins, a whole winery, a large barn and access building that was for the weddings and other events that the family had on hand, and countless other small buildings that helped the resort work.

There were two main buildings, though, that were at least three stories and gorgeous. When a storm had come through and destroyed part of it, it had been my job to restore it.

And it was still one of the highlights of my career.

The Wilder offices were on the top floor of the main building, away from the restaurant and guest rooms.

The fact that there was a large enough meeting space for every single Wilder and their families surprised me to this day. Although I knew that some companies rented it out for their private retreats.

"We're not that late," I said as I looked at my phone and cringed.

"Okay, a little late."

"I really hope there's coffee," Wyatt said.

I raised a brow. "I thought you would at least have some coffee in your system with the way that you're bouncing your toes."

Wyatt just grinned at me, that leer that made me roll my eyes.

"Oh, that perk didn't come from coffee."

"I really don't want to know what you and Ava are up to."

"Faith was at a sleepover. It was a good morning. But I'm running late."

I shoved him as he laughed, and we made our way up the stairs and into the main meeting room.

We were indeed the last ones there, although I

knew not everybody was showing up for this meeting today.

"Oh good, you're here. We have coffee," Eli said, and both Wyatt and I grinned at each other before heading over to fill up two cups.

We were a large extended family of ten, with Eliza making eleven. Eliza lived up in Colorado with her family that she had married into, and she no longer had a stake in the company. Not that she wasn't part of our family and visited often, but because she had wanted to ensure her brothers had a way to begin their lives fully. I wasn't sure of exactly everything that had occurred, but I loved Eliza and her kids. Each of my cousins and brothers was there, although none of the spouses were. I had found that odd at first, but it was Eli's wife, Alexa, who had explained what the meeting was about.

I was also grateful that my parents hadn't decided to name the four of us with the same letter. The cousins each had names that started with the letter E, and sometimes I still got the names confused.

It didn't matter that we had all grown up together and knew each other. I couldn't keep up with it. And now that everybody was having kids, I swore we needed name tags.

"You guys need to have a meeting where you discuss the family at its core. We already had the large meeting with all forty of us. Now it's time to make a decision," Eli's wife and the Wilder wedding planner had said.

So now, it was the ten of us for a meeting that I hoped would go well.

"Now that we're all here, let's talk expansion," Eli said, and I let out a breath and knew it was time.

"Are we talking about on the property or somewhere else?" Ridge asked as he leaned back in his chair.

My brother was smiling more than I'd ever known him to do so, and it made me happy to see. He put his feet up on the table. Nobody told him to remove them, and I had a feeling he hadn't even noticed he was doing it. Ridge ran security with one of the brothers-in-law, with one of the Wilder brothers-in-law, and it all was a complicated system that they seemed to figure out on their own.

"Both," Eli answered. "We haven't truly used the acreage that you guys have added. And we will once we decide if we're going to add more restaurants or more places to stay or just keep it as it is. I know we have business plans and we're ready to go with what we need there, and Brooks is going to be busy."

I lifted up my coffee. "I'm working on plans as much as I possibly can. You're just going to have to be patient," I said with a shrug.

"And frankly, I don't want to use anybody outside of our family to build," my brother Gabriel said. Gabriel was rarely here, considering he was usually out on tour with his band. But this was an important family meeting, and so we were all here together.

"We also don't want to use a company outside of Brooks. Although I know you do subcontract," Eli said.

I nodded. "Yes, I can't do everything."

"Somebody write that down. It seems like an important thing to remember," Wyatt joked. "We can engrave it on a plaque and gift it to Mom for Christmas."

I threw a balled-up napkin at him, and Ridge caught it before putting his feet down as if noticing that he was tipped back in his chair and could fall.

"We have plans for the acreage," Eli continued. "But I'm talking about the expansion that we all agreed to, but we need to discuss it one more time because it's a big endeavor."

"I'm fine with doing whatever," another cousin said. "We've already decided this as a family without just the main core Wilders."

"True, but that means that we're either going to be spread too thin or giving up responsibility. It's a big deal," Eli continued.

"We already agreed," I said with a shake of my

head. "We're going to buy up the inn and brewery that Roy, your friend, suggested. And we're going to do what we did here. Maybe not at this scale, but you're doing it for a reason. You have friends getting out of the military that need jobs. They need careers. So while we're not going to be on-site every single day, we're going to train them. And they're going to have a path. We already made this plan. I'm in to help build. Just tell me where to sign on the dotted line."

Everybody continued to speak, but in the end, we agreed.

We would be buying another parcel of land and a whole new adventure.

The Wilders were expanding and growing.

And I was going to be part of it.

Which, in the end, was good. Because it would keep me busy.

When the meeting ended, I grabbed my stuff and headed out before people could talk to me. I wasn't in the mood to deal with the line of questions that had been popping up more than usual.

Namely, trying to set me up on dates.

I didn't know what it was about married couples, but as soon as they were happy and in love and settled down, they wanted everyone else to do the same. Had I been that ridiculous when I had been married? I wasn't quite sure since my life had been wrapped around work at Amara. But no, I hoped to hell I wasn't that annoying.

I looked through my list of things to do for the day and realized that I needed something out of the supply closet. So I opened the door, walked in, and bumped into a soft body with a very familiar smell.

"Wait, don't!" Rory called out as the door closed behind me.

"Don't what?" I asked, my voice rougher than intended.

"Don't shut the door. It's stuck."

While the light was on, it was dim, as one of the bulbs had gone out. No one had told me, and we had staff to fix it, but since no one had noticed, I was going to have to do it myself.

"Are you sure you just didn't turn the handle correctly?" I asked, aware that that vanilla scent was infiltrating my nostrils, and the closet was way too small for comfort. In fact, I could feel every single curve of hers pressed to mine.

And, of course, my dick noticed.

I quickly turned so she wouldn't feel it against her stomach and tried the handle.

It didn't budge.

"I might be blonde, but I'm not an idiot. I know how to open a door."

"Well, why didn't you call someone?"

"Because my phone is in my office. Why don't you call someone?" she said.

I reached into my pocket and cursed. "My phone's in the meeting room. Fuck."

"Oh, this is great. I am so happy that my claustrophobia is getting a nice little workout today."

I frowned and turned to her, squinting in the dim light.

"You're claustrophobic?"

Her chest heaved, her breasts lifting with each deep breath, and I tried not to notice the way that her V-neck T-shirt showed every single inch of cleavage.

I swallowed hard, my mouth suddenly watering.

"Just a little bit. And you are very big, Brooks. And you're taking up way too much space."

"How long have you been in here?" I asked, my voice deep. Gruff.

"I have no idea. But could you step back?"

"My back's already to the door, Rory."

"Oh. Well. I guess the whole us avoiding each other is really going well, right?" she asked, her voice going high-pitched.

"I'm not avoiding you. I'm just staying away from you."

"I'm so glad that you cleared that up." She looked down between us and cleared her throat. "Could you really not back up because it's kind of hard to ignore a certain part of you?"

Damn, it seemed my dick ended up pressed to her stomach, and there was no alleviating that. At least, not the way we wanted to.

"Sorry, I can't control him."

"Gee, this isn't awkward at all. I'm sure someone will come searching for us soon. Or at least you. Ava doesn't know I'm here."

"Ava's at home," I whispered, my throat tight.

"Oh, crap."

The dim light wasn't bright enough for me to see every inch of her, but just enough so I could see those plump lips and the way that she practically shivered in my hold.

Without thinking, I slid one hand around her waist and the other over her ponytail. I tugged slightly and her mouth parted.

"Brooks."

"Just shut up."

"Don't tell me to shut up. You shut up."

"Fine," I growled.

And then I crushed my mouth to hers.

I pulled on her ponytail, hard, and she gasped into my mouth as I licked along the seam of her lips. She once again parted for me, kissing me back with as much fervor.

She tasted of mint, coffee, and everything Rory.

I moved into her, grinding myself against her as she slid her hands up the back of my shirt, nails digging into my skin.

I deepened the kiss, practically devouring her as I did the one thing I promised myself I would never do.

I kissed Rory Thompson once again.

And she kissed me back.

And when I finally wrenched myself from her, ready to come in my jeans like a teenager, we both stood there, panting.

"That didn't happen," I rumbled.

"The problem is...it did."

And when one of the cleaning staff opened the door behind me, Rory practically shoved me out of the way and ran. And I stood with my back to the doorway, wondering what the hell I had just done.

CHAPTER TWO
RORY

How many penises did this Minotaur have? I shook my head and looked back at my notes, nodding that the author in question did indeed request *two* penises. Or was it penisi? I also marked down the title of the novel again, so I'd remember to read this book when it released because I wanted to know if a Minotaur ended up with new characters or maybe there was going to be a little fun later with both of them. Or maybe I really needed to step away from my drawing board and take a walk.

A smile playing on my face, I clicked through to my next request, making sure that my calendar was up to date. I was my own boss, and that meant sometimes I had to be malicious to myself in order to get things done.

It was funny to think that nearly five years ago, I had been working full-time for another company, drawing exactly what they told me to, stifling my creativity, and yet thirsting for more within that job sphere because that's what I thought you needed to do. But as a digital graphic artist and illustrator, that meant sometimes I got to dive into drawings I would never have thought of. And it meant that I added to my TBR.

Next on my list was a drawing for another for a book box. They would use the character and setting art for numerous items, and readers would be happy. Then later in the day, my project was for the series that had allowed me to be self-employed.

A children's series about a young boy, his goat friend, and raw apples that had saved the world.

I, of course, did that art under a different name because a website with both of those in my portfolio didn't really go well for some clients.

My lips twitched, and I penciled off something else in my calendar, knowing that we might be on book thirteen in this children's series, but the consultations for books fourteen and fifteen were coming up soon.

If I worked for a publisher or the author themselves, each timeline was different, but I didn't mind. That just meant I could spend a little more time with my spread-sheets and calendars.

It was funny because most people thought since my job had mostly to do with art, that I had to be the ditzy woman who had to thrive in art and only focused on drawing. That none of the analytical side of my brain would be useful.

At least that's what the one serious boyfriend I'd ever had had thought.

Even my sister had told me that a few times until we had both backed off and settled into our relationship. She had been the bright star, the logical mind who had thrived in math and science.

I had indeed been the artsy one who liked history and English, but I had been good at everything, at least good enough to get straight A's just like her.

I rubbed my fist over my chest, wondering why I was thinking about Beth.

It had been at least a week since I had thought about my sister and the pain that came with the fact that I hadn't spoken to her in six years.

I frowned as I looked at my calendar, at the color-coded projects lined up for the next few months.

Six years. That couldn't be right. That meant it had been six years since I had laughed and joked with my big sister. No, that wasn't even right. Because it had been long before that time since we had truly laughed with each other. And even though I called her my big sister, it was only because she had beaten me by three minutes.

My twin, the woman who was the other half of my soul, had cut me out of her life with a scalpel and had done the same for everyone else in her past life. Any connections to the world that weren't from her husband's influence had been shorn away without a backward glance.

She hadn't even shown up for our parents' funeral four years prior. I knew that the funeral company and hospital had contacted her, but she had ignored my calls and emails. And it wasn't as if I even knew where she and her husband Nolan lived. Where the girls lived.

I got up from my desk and began to pace. Cameron would be what, twelve now? Alice, seven. I had barely even held Alice as an infant before she had been ripped from my arms by Nolan, the man overbearing and asshole-ish like usual.

I still didn't know what my twin had seen in him, but she had fallen head over heels for Nolan Roberts and inch-by-inch had been turned into a person I hadn't recognized.

I let out a shaky breath and tasted salt on my tongue.

"Damn it, Rory," I growled at myself as I furiously wiped away my tears. I hadn't even realized I was crying until the tears were down my cheeks, and here I was once again, trying to remember a woman who didn't want me in her life. She hadn't agreed with my lifestyle, a single woman who had sex before marriage and had even lived with a man for six months. Ben and I had been serious enough to live together but not serious enough to get married. I had bored him and had dealt with too much drama, according to him. Which, I always felt contradicted each other.

Either I could have too much drama, or I could be boring. I couldn't be both.

Yet Ben had thought so. Because I had been boring in bed, boring when it came to my goals. Boring in my job. And dull and lackluster.

But far too much drama with my twin sister joining, not necessarily a cult, but something so cult-like that I had been cut out.

Shamed and forgotten.

I swallowed hard, shook my head, and went back to my desk.

I had art to work on, countless emails to go through, and I needed to finally hire an assistant to help me with social media and other projects.

I'd gained enough popularity in certain circles that now I needed someone to help deal with administrative tasks so I could focus on the art.

"That didn't sound very boring, did it Ben?" I mumbled.

Then I set aside all thoughts of the man who hadn't loved me enough to figure out who I was, and the man that, frankly, I realized I hadn't loved at all. We had both been at fault. Because honestly, he was just as boring.

I opened up my current project, lifted my stylus, and got to work.

While I sometimes worked with pencils and paint, at that moment, digital art was the best for me. I could focus on exactly what I needed to for these types of projects, and not get bogged down with messiness and my indecisiveness of certain mediums.

Sometimes though, the media needed to change for the project because I got too far into my head.

Currently however, the couple in a romantic tango, fully clothed for this project, shone brightly on my screen.

I worked on shading her dress, knowing that I was going to have to pick up this book as well. Usually, I had on an audiobook as I did this, but today I needed music that pounded out of the speakers and let me not think.

Because, at first, it had nothing to do with my sister or my ex or life in general. No, they didn't earn my headspace or thoughts.

Brooks.

I forced myself to unclench my fingers around the stylus, not realizing that I had tensed until pain ricocheted up my pointer finger.

While I wasn't sure if Brooks remembered every single moment of that night in an airport hotel, I did. Because I had only been partially drunk. I had consented just as much as he had. But he had blocked it out enough to never speak of it. And I remembered every taste, every orgasm, and the fact that it had been the best sex of my life on one of the worst nights of my life.

Because my parents' ashes had been spread over the ocean hours before and I wasn't sure how I was supposed to move on from that.

My parents had each died from an upper respiratory infection that had taken a toll. It had been a very bad case throughout the country, and mostly children had died from it, but in this case, my parents hadn't been able to push through, and their lungs had stopped working. Their oxygen had gone so low that each of them had been intubated, and I had sat in a waiting room, waiting for them to wake up. And they never had.

I could still remember the look of confusion in my mom's gaze, and the look of knowing in my father's.

Because they knew eventually, that neither one of them was ever going to wake up.

Once again, I wiped the tears on my cheeks, annoyed with myself. My parents had made end-of-life decisions, and I had been the executor of their will. After all, Beth had cut them out of their lives as well. They hadn't cut her out of their will. But I was the one who had made the choices. I was the one who worked on their funerals. Had spoken to their friends and family and uncles and aunts and everyone else in our extended family that we weren't close to but had come to give their respects.

And Beth hadn't.

So that night, I tried to drink away my pain, wondering if I should just get on a different plane and head somewhere that had nothing to do with family.

It hadn't helped that I had also been fired that morning because they'd wanted to cut back and use interns for my job.

I huffed and continued to draw, annoyed with myself for going down this memory lane. Of course, I knew exactly why I was thinking of that night. Because he had kissed me again. No, maybe I had kissed him?

I wasn't sure exactly which had been the case, but in the end, his hand had been in my hair, pulling just hard enough. It had made my toes curl. And he had been rough that night, leaving bruises exactly where I had wanted them, and yet tender in ways I hadn't thought possible.

And just that taste had brought it all back to the surface, and I knew I was an idiot.

It was my own fault for working at the Wilder Retreat. It was my own fault for thinking that that place happened to be the most peaceful place when I needed to clear my thoughts and work and not think about family or stress or money or life.

Part of me hated the fact that anything having to do with a Wilder calmed me. Because Brooks Wilder had nothing to do with calm.

It was just my luck that my best friend, the person who knew every single thing about me except that night, happened to be married to his brother.

Fate truly hated me sometimes. As if I had conjured her, my phone buzzed, and I looked down at an incoming call from Ava.

Distractions already pushing through the day, I set down my work and answered.

"Hey there, bestie," I said, trying to sound as if I hadn't been crying.

"What's wrong?" she asked, that fiery tone comforting.

"Just drawing."

"That doesn't actually answer my question, babe."

"I hate that you can read me so well. I was just thinking about Mom and Dad and life. And then I was crying, and now I'm getting back to work. You know, typical Thursday."

It wasn't quite a lie, but it wasn't the whole truth. Thankfully, she wasn't in front of me, so she wasn't able to realize that.

"I'm so sorry, hon. Do you want me to come over? We can have tea and talk about boys."

I snorted, knowing that that was the last thing that I wanted. Not that I didn't love my best friend, but I wasn't about to talk about boys. Because the only boy I wanted to think about these days was the one I couldn't and shouldn't have.

"There aren't any boys to speak of, my friend. Unless we talk about yours. And unlike some of the Wilders, you don't share yours."

One of the Wilder cousins was married to not only a woman, but a man, and the three of them were in the most adorable and sexiest poly relationship I had ever known.

"Sorry, he's all mine. I don't share. I'm very territorial."

"And Wyatt isn't territorial at all," I teased.

"Well, there was this one time—"

"Nope," I cut her off. "I do not want to know. You keep your sexy stories about your man to yourself. Unless we're drinking Wilder Wine."

"Meanie," she teased. I shook my head and laughed, leaving my office in my small two-bedroom apartment and heading towards the tiny rally kitchen. I'd rented it from a decent landlord, and they were nice to me, but things were getting a little shoddy. I made decent enough money that I could rent a larger place, but part of me kept waiting to find a home. One that I could buy and put down roots in.

One that would have space for Beth and her family when they visited.

Another stab to the heart.

Because they wouldn't be visiting.

"Anyway, I'm calling because we have practice coming up and games all weekend. Are you going to be there, or are you going to take this weekend off from little kids' soccer," she asked.

I smiled before going to the tap to wash out my tea kettle. "Maisie is adorable in her little uniform. I should be able to make it. As long as I get caught up on work tonight and tomorrow, I'll be on schedule, and then I can be her loudest cheering squad."

"You could try, but we all know the Wilders are going to be louder."

"That's true. Damn it," I grumbled as the faucet refused to turn off completely.

"What's wrong?" Ava asked, alert.

"My stupid faucet keeps leaking, and I can't fix it. And it annoys me because my landlord said he would fix it and he hasn't, and I have a wrench. I know how to do these things. But I think it's the actual faucet itself. And I can't replace it since it's not mine."

"And the landlord's not coming over at all?" Ava asked, annoyance in her tone.

"He said he would. But he has countless other things to do," I griped. "It's okay. I'll fix it. Eventually. I'll just put something under it so I can collect the water and not waste it."

"I'll send Brooks over."

"No!" I called out and realized I screamed it into the phone.

Ava was silent for so long that I had no idea what she was thinking.

"I mean, no. You don't need to send out one of your brother-in-laws to help me. I can handle it."

"He also can help. East is working on another project out by Austin, or I would send him. But Brooks is right in my house at the moment talking with Wyatt. Let me just ask him."

"It's really okay. He's a contractor. He builds homes for a living. He's not a plumber."

"You're allowed to ask for help."

"I do know that. You're my best friend. I ask you all the time."

"Whatever," Ava mumbled.

"Ava Wilder, don't you dare."

"Oh, I am daring. Love you, bye!" Ava said, and the phone clicked off.

"She wouldn't," I mumbled. "Oh, she would."

I looked around my tiny apartment, knowing it wasn't shabby per se, but it wasn't as beautiful as any of the homes that the Wilders lived in. Brooks had even built a few, and they were gorgeous masterpieces that my mouth watered over.

The problem, however, wasn't him seeing me in a tiny apartment that I could afford easily. No, it was the fact that my mouth watered for him too.

I looked in the mirror over the sink, cursing that I had a messy bun on the top of my head, blue light glasses, and a coffee stain on my shirt.

I set my tea kettle on its stand, knowing that my afternoon tea was going to have to wait.

I wouldn't have time to shower because Ava would probably force Brooks to drop everything he was doing and help me now, if he even agreed to it, and I quickly stripped off my shirt and leggings, nearly tripped over my feet, and ran to my bedroom.

I tossed my dirty clothes in the hamper and pulled on jeans that were a little snug over my wide hips, but I didn't mind. They made me look hot.

Wait, why was I looking hot for Brooks?

Damn it.

I thought about taking them off and putting on a dress that was a little boxy, but then I would think about what I was wearing under the dress and... why was I acting like this? I had lasted two years now being in the same room with Brooks without acting like a weirdo. Two years where I focused on work and trying to be his friend. Where we acted awkward, but hopefully not so awkward that anyone noticed. In fact, no one had even mentioned it. Not even Ava, who I knew had noticed something at that first meeting. But she had been so lost in her issues with Wyatt at the time that, maybe, she had forgotten.

I had lasted two years like this; I could do it longer.

I quickly put on a black three-quarters-length top, slid my feet into shoes so that way I wouldn't be barefoot when he was walking around in work boots, and went to my desk.

I would just continue to work, and then he wouldn't show up.

And everything would be fine.

Of course, nothing was fine.

The doorbell rang, and I nearly jumped out of my skin, setting my stylus down again. It had been 40 minutes since the call, and I had finally gotten back to work.

I quickly turned off my music and went to my door, telling myself I was an idiot.

When I opened the door, Brooks stood there, scowl on his face, and that chiseled jaw of his making it hard to breathe.

He was as tall as any of the Wilders, at least over six foot. Broad-shouldered, narrow waist, thick thighs, and a very thick cock.

No, I was not going to think about that.

It was just my luck that the sexiest man alive, with those haunted blue eyes that sometimes looked gray when he was truly angry or feeling an emotion I couldn't touch or taste. His nose had a slight bump in it where he must have broken it before, and his jaw was cut from granite itself. Right now it was covered in a light beard, meaning he hadn't shaved for a few days.

It was longer than it had been when it had been a little rough against my skin, and I had left that utility closet with a slight beard burn.

Not that anyone had noticed because I had run to

my car and hidden at my apartment until I could breathe again.

And yet, I wasn't breathing now.

"Ava said you needed help?" he asked, that gruff voice going straight down my spine.

"I'm really sorry for this. I can handle it on my own, I promise."

"Is your landlord that shitty?" he asked as he looked around the small apartment and cursed under his breath. "Sorry. I've had a morning. But I really don't mind fixing your faucet, Rory."

Just the sound of my name on his tongue made me want to weep.

Because he never called me Rory. We never called each other by the other's name.

We were so good about pretending we didn't know each other that it felt as if I had him etched on my soul.

And how stupidly poetic was that?

I cleared my throat, knowing I was staring now, and took a step back.

"He helps with a lot of things, but while he's nice, he's slow. And I've tried to fix it myself, but it just leaks for a good 10 minutes or longer after I use it."

"It might need to be replaced, Rory."

"That's what I told Ava. But I'm not allowed to replace things like that. Not without his permission,

47

but he says he can fix it. So it's a cycle where here I am."

"Let's see what I can do, okay? Maybe I can get a little more use out of it so you can wait for your so-called nice landlord to take care of it."

"This is very much beneath your pay grade, Brooks," I said as I gestured towards the small galley kitchen past my living room. The place wasn't too large. It had two bathrooms, thankfully, but the second bathroom was in the hall, not part of the room I had made my office. The closets were practically non-existent, so I'd filled my love of clothes in wardrobes that were disguised as other pieces of furniture in the apartment.

It wasn't much, but it was mine.

"Come on, I'll help. It's not a big deal."

"And yet Ava pushed you out here for it. I'm sorry."

"Stop apologizing for my sister-in-law. She did that puppy dog face, and frankly, I needed to get out of their house before she tried to set me up on another date," he grumbled.

I tripped over my feet, an odd sense of hurt slamming through me.

That didn't make any sense. Why would I feel such betrayal at Ava for setting him up on dates? She didn't know that I had accidentally fallen mildly into obsession with Brooks.

I had kept that secret from her, and she wanted everybody to be happy.

"She tries to set me up as well. And I'm not very good at it."

My mouth went dry as he turned to study my face.

"I don't let her set me up at all," he whispered.

I didn't know why relief was the first emotion I felt.

I was in so much trouble.

"Well, I won't hover. I will be appreciative, but I don't want to bother you. There's not a lot of space in here."

"Your apartment's fine, Rory. Stop acting like you should be ashamed of it. You shouldn't. It's a good area."

"I'm saving for a house. And I hate moving so I've just stayed in this apartment way past time," I said honestly.

"I hate moving too, hence why I build things and try not to leave."

"And I can do some home repairs, but not a lot. And that's why being a homeowner scares me."

"And your landlord should be doing more then."

My phone buzzed again, and I looked down at the readout, not recognizing the number but it didn't say spam, so maybe it was something important. I constantly had phone calls from publishers and other places that I worked with, including printers.

"Go ahead and take that. I've got this."

His gaze caught mine again, and so I wrenched my attention away and answered.

"Hello."

"Is this Rory Thompson?" a deep voice asked, and I frowned.

"This is. How can I help you?"

"Ms. Thompson, this is the Franklin Police Department, and I regret to—"

I knew he was saying more words. Knew there was something important to be explained.

But my knees went out from beneath me, and then Brooks was there, holding me up as my world ended, and I told myself I couldn't break. Not again.

CHAPTER THREE
BROOKS

I had moved to be closer to my family, and I had done it knowing full well I would be spending more time with people than without. Right after Amara had died, I had buried myself in work and tried to ensure to the world—including my parents and brothers—that I could handle being alone. That while grieving, I wasn't going to go off the deep end. I'd only had one bad night of drinking, and of course, look how that had ended.

So when I had been summoned to a family meeting, I wasn't surprised that while you could beg off if you wanted to, there had been enough urgency in the tone that I was now sitting here in my cousin Eli's larger-than-life home that I had helped him build, wondering how I had made this my problem.

"There's so much paperwork for her to deal with, and she's not letting me help at all. And I know that Rory can do this on her own. I know she says that, at least, but we all know that there's going to be a thousand little things that need to be done," Ava rambled as she paced in front of us.

Most of the Wilders had come through here to try to figure out how to help Rory out of an impossible situation.

When Rory had nearly collapsed in my arms at that phone call, she had tried to push me away, but I had ignored her. Instead, I had held her up by her elbow as she steeled herself and listened to what had turned out to be the authorities on the other end of the line.

"So her brother-in-law was flying the plane, and it just went down?" Aurora asked as she slid her hand into my brother Ridge's grip.

"That's what the guy said," I grumbled, trying not to picture exactly what had washed over Rory's face when she had heard the news that her sister and brother-in-law had died in a small plane crash, leaving behind two little girls, a mountain of debt thanks to different state laws, and a group of people who did not want to relinquish rights to anything Beth and Nolan might have left that had value.

I didn't know Rory's family, and I didn't want to know them. All I knew from hearsay at this point was that Rory and her sister hadn't gotten along recently, and she hadn't seen her nieces in years.

Hell, from what it looked like, the rest of my family knew more about Rory than I had. But that was understandable. I had done my best to ignore everything about her for long enough. So the only thing that I knew was what she tasted like, and the fact that she drew pictures for a living.

I tried my best not to know anything else.

I was seriously an asshole.

"Yes, apparently her brother-in-law Nolan was flying and had a pilot's license. The two of them were going to some other retreat as part of their group." Ava shivered. "Honestly, from the way that Rory explained the group, it sounds more like a cult than a community, but her sister and brother-in-law were higher up in the community's power structure and were able to borrow the company plane. It was engine failure, and the authorities don't think it was tampered with. It was just bad luck."

"I hate the idea that that would be bad luck," Wyatt grumbled.

Of my brothers, Ridge and Wyatt had been able to

come, Gabriel and Briar were out on tour again with his band.

My cousins Eli, Evan, and Elijah were here. Everett and his wife were out in L.A. at their house there, while East and Elliott and their spouses were keeping the retreat running while we could have this meeting. I still didn't know why exactly I had been invited, but since I had been the one to call Ava when Rory hadn't, I guess I was part of this.

Even though I wanted nothing to do with it.

"And she doesn't have any other family?" Aurora asked, wiping away tears. "That's so terrible."

"There are a few aunts and uncles that are distant, but yes, the only family that Rory has are her two nieces. And now, according to what Rory said, she was in the will as their guardian."

"How old are the kids?" Alexis asked as she leaned into Eli's side. Their two children were upstairs, napping, along with Kendall and Evan's kids. Elijah's and Maddie's kids were with the nanny at their place since I knew that they were trying to see if they could make a nanny work. With all of us working full-time jobs, Wilder childcare was now a thing we cared about.

It was odd to think that though I had been the first to get married, I hadn't ended up with children. Amara and I had wanted to start right away, but the cancer had come first.

And there had been no time for children when we had been trying every clinical trial out there to save her.

"Brooks, are you listening?" Ava asked as she blinked at me.

I shook myself out of my memories and frowned. "No," I said, and Wyatt snorted.

"At least you're honest," my brother grumbled.

"Sorry. My mind was wandering. What's wrong?"

"Cameron's twelve, Alice is seven." Ava shook her head. "Right now she's at her apartment, and while we did our best to make the guest bedroom no longer an office and a space for the girls, there's just not enough space. I was looking at rentals for her, but I just don't know what to do. There's got to be something we can do to help. She hates taking help."

It had only been eighteen hours since I had left Rory in Ava's arms after I had called my sister-in-law to come to the apartment. I hadn't said a damn thing, just stood there next to Rory as she shook, trying to comprehend the other line of that phone call.

There would be paperwork to deal with, and she'd need to fly out there and meet the children, but I hadn't known what the hell I was supposed to do. So I'd run.

And yet, here I was, at the meeting.

"It's all just so terrible," Aurora said after a moment. "Their parents are gone, and they don't even know their aunt. Do you know why Rory and her sister were estranged?"

I looked at Ava, honestly curious.

While I did my best to stay out of Rory's way, the fact that Rory and her sister were so estranged to the point that she hadn't seen them in years was a curiosity.

"It all has to do with that community they joined."

"A cult?" Eli asked.

"I don't know if we can precisely say it's a cult, but it felt like that. They both worked within the constructs of it and had risen to the upper echelons. Hence why they could borrow that plane," Ava explained. "They were going to a retreat, and I don't know all the details. But she hasn't seen them in six years."

I did the math, realizing that maybe there was a reason she had been drinking as much as I had that night.

No. I didn't want to know more about Rory. Because part of me always wanted to know more about her. There was a reason I had stayed away, and it wasn't that I didn't like her.

It was that she reminded me of something that I

wanted too much. Something I craved. And I wouldn't be having that.

"When's the funeral?" Aurora asked.

"Tomorrow," Ava growled, and I narrowed my gaze.

"So is she going to the funeral then?" I bit out. Did she not want to? Or were others making it difficult for her?

"She's not invited," Ava said pointedly. "Because while she is a guardian of the children, the will clearly states that the community gets everything. They're going to organize the funeral, the remains, take the house, all funds, possessions. Everything that wasn't in those little girls' rooms goes straight to the community."

"Are you fucking serious?" I burst out as the rest of them all spoke over one another, wondering how the hell that could happen.

"Is that even legal?" I asked.

"It sure seems like it," Ava said as she wiped away tears. Wyatt pulled her in close, and she nuzzled into him.

"All I know is that she's not going to be there to say goodbye to her sister, and she's trying to get out there as soon as she can to see the girls and bring them back here."

"To a place that they don't know and away from

people that they've grown up with," Aurora said softly. "That's got to be terrible and such a burden on all of them."

"Is the community going to fight for the kids?" I asked, wondering exactly what kind of community this was.

Ava shook her head. "It hasn't even been a day, and they've already explained in explicit terms that they won't fight for custody if she doesn't fight the will for anything else. And from what I can see, they have the money to make it a bloodbath."

"So she's going to bring them here. Because I'm pretty sure none of us want those kids anywhere near them," I growled.

Ava met my gaze, and I knew she had questions. Hell, anyone who saw me around Rory had questions. It surprised me, though, that it had taken this long for Ava to even look at me in that way.

"She's not going to be gone for long, and she's going to bring those girls back home, and she's not letting me go with her."

Wyatt ran his hand up and down Ava's arm. "Those girls are already going to be seeing a stranger in their aunt. Maybe seeing another stranger would be too much."

"But that doesn't mean she's alone when everybody

gets here," Alexis put in. "We Wilders are a loud bunch, and while Rory technically isn't a Wilder, we adopted her long ago. She's a Wilder woman for wine night, at least, so she's one of us. What can we do?" She pulled out her planner and pen, and my lips nearly twitched at that thought.

Because while a sense of grief and confusion seemed overwhelming to the rest of us, we apparently were going to make plans.

"How is she going to fit two kids in her tiny apartment?" I asked as they went over supplies and schools and paperwork for the girls.

Everyone stared at me, and I shrugged. "Her office is in her guest room, and there's already not enough space for her to walk around. Is she going to look for another rental? Are you guys going to put her in one of the cabins on the property?"

"Rory isn't going to take handouts from us, at least not something that big," Ava said slowly. "As it is it's going to take guilt and pressure in order for her to let us help with the paperwork that it's going to take for the move. Because I don't know exactly what those little girls are going to need, but we're going to make sure they have everything."

"Damn straight," Aurora said as Ridge squeezed her shoulder.

"We're not going to be able to bring their parents back, or help any of the hurts, but we can make sure that they have a pillow to sleep on and people around so they know they're not alone."

"And we won't be so cult-like," Kendall pointed out. "And I know people joke that the Wilders can be, but what the hell is this community?"

"All I know is if that community comes after those kids, they're going to have to face us," I blurted, and people once again stared at me. "What? I don't like the sound of them."

"Same here," Elijah said as he looked through his phone. "Oh, and we have lawyers, too, so we'll ensure that we can take any necessary steps to guarantee it's not an issue."

"I don't think it will be," Ava put in. "I think once the girls are here, they're going to cut ties. At least, that's what Rory felt. It just feels icky."

Wyatt leaned forward. "Okay, so let's find them a place to stay and figure out how to get Rory to agree to move."

I shook my head and stood up, pulling my phone out of my pocket. "You know what, fuck it. I'll deal with it."

Everyone gaped at me. "What?"

"What do you mean by you'll deal with it?" Wyatt

asked slowly, looking as if I'd lost my mind. Maybe I had.

"The house next door to mine is open. My renters moved out, so there's enough space for everyone. And it's in a good school district, close enough so Rory can drive them both. Though, I don't really know what grades they will be in."

"That's a brilliant idea," Ava said as she stood up. "Rory's going to hate it, but maybe I can convince her. And that'll ensure that she's close enough to all of us, and you'll be right next door to help her if she needs anything. It's perfect."

I didn't like the odd look on her face, one that said she had something else up her sleeve, or maybe I was just thinking too hard.

I shook my head, though. "No. I'll handle it. I'll make sure she does what we need her to. You guys handle all the rest. I'll make sure she has a place to come home to."

And with that, I walked out, leaving everybody flabbergasted. They called after me, but I ignored them.

I needed to head to Rory's and make another fucking terrible decision when it came to her.

My hands tightened on the steering wheel as I drove towards Rory's small apartment, wondering what the hell I was doing. But for the life of me I couldn't think about three people in that tiny apartment, trying to navigate a new world. I knew firsthand what it was like when your world broke into a thousand pieces.

Because those little girls would be grieving and would have no idea what the hell they were doing. And I knew that Rory wouldn't be grieving at all. She would be pushing it down, working on a checklist like everybody else, and she would do her best to think of the girls and not of the fact that she had just lost her sister.

I couldn't do much, and I didn't want to do anything else, but I could do this.

I was already out of the car and walking up her steps before I thought better of it. I knocked as quietly as I could, but I was a big man, and it sounded more like a pounding than anything.

Rory pulled open the door, eyes wide. "What are you doing here Brooks?"

I studied her face, the dark circles, the paleness. But her eyes weren't puffy and her cheeks weren't red. She hadn't cried other than those few tears that had fallen after the first phone call. She was going to break, and I didn't know what the hell I would do when that happened.

Wait. Why would that matter? It wasn't as if I was going to be there when it happened. Rory wasn't mine. I had already dealt with losing somebody before. I wasn't going to deal with losing somebody else again. Let alone someone who was clearly dealing with things that were way too much for me.

"Here. Take these." I held out my hand, and Rory looked down at it, confused.

"Brooks. What are you doing here? I'm exhausted, and I'm trying to figure out how to get the girls here because I don't know how much stuff they have."

I shook my head. "Let Ava help. You know the Wilders already have a fucking spreadsheet going."

She blinked. "What?" Then she realized I was standing in her doorway and gestured me inside. "Come inside. I don't need my neighbors to hear everything. What are you saying?"

"Let Ava help when she calls you. Or hell, when she comes over. Just let her help."

"Brooks. I don't know what you're talking about."

"You know your best friend. She's going to want to help. They've got plans. You be there for the girls. Now take these." I held out my fist again, and she still frowned.

"What are they?"

"Keys." I dropped them in her open palm, her eyes wide.

"Keys for what?"

"I own five homes. I built them and I rent them out. I live in one of them, and the one next door is open right now. It's a four-bedroom, meaning the girls can either share or have their own, I don't know what the hell girls their ages do. But you can have your own room, and there can be a guest room or an office or whatever you need. I know the area well, and Ava and the others can help you. But just don't think too hard. You're not going to be able to fit the girls in here. Take my keys."

I stood there, heart in my throat, wondering what the hell I was doing. I hadn't even spoken in complete sentences and was now asking the person I tried to stay away from to move next door to me.

"But, no, we'll be fine here." Her cheeks pinked in a pretty blush, and I shoved that thought away. "And I don't need your charity."

"You can pay rent. I don't fucking care. But what I do care about is the fact that I have the space, and you need it. Just let someone help you for once."

Her eyes narrowed, finally an emotion other than bleakness filling that gaze. "You know what? That's rich, Brooks."

"Just move in. The others will help you with it. I'm leaving tomorrow because I need to set up the expansion. I'll be over an hour away for the next few weeks." I hadn't really wanted to leave tomorrow, but frankly, I needed to get out of here. I needed to breathe and focus on something else.

Not the fact that I had just asked my worst and best fantasy to live next door to me.

Not to mention, an anniversary I didn't want to think about was coming up, and I would rather be away from my family for that than have to deal with any pitying or worrying looks.

"You can't just give me a house."

"I can. We can talk about paperwork and whatever you need later. But those girls are going to need a place to sleep. And you don't need to stress about other things out of your control. Just take it."

"Brooks. I don't know what to say."

I reached out without conscious thought, my fingers sliding along her jaw. She froze and leaned into the touch. I stood there, feeling her soft skin against my rough calluses, and sighed.

"I'm so damn sorry, Rory."

"Me too. Me too." She let out a deep breath, then finally rolled her shoulders back, so I let my hand drop. "Okay. I guess we do need the space. Thank you, Brooks."

I just shook my head and wondered what the hell I was doing.

I'd needed to help her. Every part of me needed

that. I couldn't give her anything else, but I could give her space. At least for the girls. Because now I would be their landlord. Their neighbor.

And there wasn't enough space in the world for me to figure out what to do with that.

CHAPTER FOUR
RORY

How could the world end and rebuild so many times in only a month?

Time lied.

Grief lied.

And those who said grief could calm after time lied.

It was as if grief were the slow movements of a clock. As if each tick of the minute hand, each swipe of the hour hand would forever slow to a crawl because you were the one who wanted it to move.

Those people had never found themselves a caretaker to two children who wanted nothing to do with you.

Because time didn't slow to a crawl. It slapped you in the face with reality, wondering where the hell you had been this entire time. Then, it would freeze in place. It didn't even have the decency to crawl.

It had been a month since my world had rocked on its axis one more time. And I didn't think I had anything left in me for it to rock again.

One month since my sister and brother-in-law had died. One month since I had dropped everything to pick up the girls from the only home they had ever known and ripped them away from it.

One month since I'd only had one option when it came to those girls: take them home, away from the community that wanted nothing to do with them now that their parents were gone, and never ask for more.

One month, and I didn't even know if grief had a name because I was too busy drowning in everything else.

"I hate it here. You can't make me stay here."

I didn't say anything. Didn't nod or explain to the child in front of me that yelling wasn't going to accomplish anything. In fact, the only thing that yelling did was give me a headache. And I wasn't even allowed to yell back.

Part of me wanted to go back in time and apologize to my parents for every time I had rolled my eyes, sneered, and told my parents I hated them. Because I had been a brat. Maybe not as much of a brat as others were, but I hadn't cared for my parents as much as I had needed to, especially in the face of a twelve-year-old's inarguable hatred.

"I don't know why we couldn't have stayed home. Then I could be with my friends. Not here with you. Mom didn't even like you. Where were you all these years?"

Cameron, my beautiful, ferocious, and brilliant twelve-year-old niece continued to lob insults at me as if she weren't cutting me with a blade with each and every spoken word.

"I hate it here. There's nothing to do. It's all brown and gross, and I don't have any friends here. I hate it here. And I hate you."

"Cameron. I'm so sorry that we had to move here. That everything has changed so quickly. I know it's not easy, but I'm doing everything in my power to make sure the transition is at least something we can bear together."

I wasn't good with words. I drew pictures having to do with books and other people's words. How was I supposed to find a way to aid Cameron's grief when I couldn't even focus on what would make sense. What would help.

Cameron might be twelve years old, but she was nearly as tall as me. My sister had always been tall, it hadn't mattered that we were twins, we were fraternal. Meaning though we looked identical in our facial features, she had sprouted four inches compared to me. And my brother-in-law was well over six feet. In fact, he was about the size of a Wilder. I pushed the idea that I would use a Wilder as a comparison from my mind. Because while the Wilders had dropped everything to help me, I couldn't focus on them right then. I had to focus on the little girl who was breaking in front of me.

"I hate you," Cameron spat again.

"That's fine. You can hate me right now, but I can't change certain things. I want to. I want to go back in time and fix this, but I can't. But we're all in this together, Cameron. You're not alone. You're going to start school soon, and you can find new people."

"I don't want new friends. I had them. Until you took me away."

How was I supposed to tell her that if I hadn't, I would've had some form of a custody battle on my hands? It didn't matter that I was the one in the will; the community had far-reaching lawyers and friends themselves. I had done what I thought was best, and that was bringing them to my family that I had created with Ava and the others.

I was even in Brooks's spare home. Because

somehow he had had a space for me when I hadn't had any space for these little girls.

Cameron pulled back her shoulder-length blonde hair and tugged on it. "I just want to go home."

"We are home now, dummy," Alice said from my side. Her bright strawberry-blonde hair fell to the middle of her back in glorious curls. She had freckles on her nose and probably would never be as tall as Cameron. No, she had gotten her height from my side of the family, specifically my mother's. She also had rosy cheeks and looked like a little angel.

And while Cameron had dove into her grief with hate and finding me a good punching bag, Alice bounced between a million different emotions at once.

She was only seven, but the mind behind those dewy gray eyes was of at least a 40-year-old.

When she wasn't calling her sister names, she was off in her own little world of make-believe, constantly following me around the large home that didn't feel like my own.

Cameron had resorted to ice and building a wall for herself.

While Alice had become a stage-five clinger, who wouldn't let me out of her sight. Thankfully, I worked from home, but even then, I knew we would have to nip this in the bud at some point.

She didn't cling to the others who visited, as the Wilder women had been by daily to make sure that we had help, but Alice only left my sight if she wanted to go to the backyard and play make-believe in stories of her own.

Maybe stories in which her mom and dad were alive, and she wasn't forced to live with her evil aunt.

Okay, perhaps I was placing Cameron's visage on my own, but what else was I supposed to think?

It had been a month of constant fighting, tears, and figuring out what we were supposed to do.

And I was failing. Failing to the point that I knew if I didn't find my feet soon, I was going to lose everything.

My phone buzzed again, and I ignored it. I was a week behind on work, which, in the grand scheme of things, wasn't too bad, but as my own boss, I needed to get back on track. I had three mouths to feed now, and that meant I couldn't think about my future the way I had been.

To think, I had been worried about being too close to Brooks, wondering if I was going to be alone until the end of time.

Now I would never be alone. There would be two little girls who constantly needed me, and I had no idea how to do this mom thing.

But I wasn't a mom. I was an aunt. An aunt who

hadn't been allowed to be near these two their entire lives. And now I was somehow supposed to raise them to be good people. I was already failing.

"Cameron. I know you don't like it here. I know everything is terrible. But you can't yell at me like that."

Again, I didn't know how to do this parenting thing. I knew I shouldn't allow her to yell at me, to scream, to call me names, or say that she hated me. But I wasn't sure how to be the disciplinarian. I didn't even know this girl. She was nothing like the gap-toothed child that I had last seen. I still couldn't come to terms with the fact that my sister had taken them from me. Had joined her not-quite-a-cult and had ripped them from my life. But wishes and thinking of the past weren't going to help anything.

Especially not now.

"And Alice, don't call your sister names."

"I'm sorry," Alice said quickly, her eyes filling with tears. She wrapped her arm around my waist, and I held her close, running my hand through those soft, nearly pink curls.

"Oh, I see how it is. You love her more than me. Why? Because she looks more like you? And I look more like my mom? My mom that you didn't even love."

I nearly staggered back at the venom in her tone. Because nothing of what she said was correct. I had loved my sister. I still did. Even when I hated what she had done and would never understand the why of it. I loved her.

And, considering my sister and I were twins, the only thing that had been different was our heights. Her saying that I looked like Alice versus her made no sense.

But the preteen was trying to find things to hate about me, and now she was reaching for anything she could.

I was already so tired, and I didn't know what I was supposed to do now.

"Cameron. School starts soon, and I know that we have all of the paperwork and lists, thanks to Miss Alexis. Why don't we go through those and then we can go shopping for what you need."

"I don't want to go to school. Not in some hick town."

I nearly crossed my eyes because although we were in a small town, we were right at the edge of the district where she would be going to a larger school than she had at her old home. But explaining that once again would only lead to more tantrums. And I didn't know if I had that in me.

"Cameron. We need to pick out the rest of your school things."

She would be starting seventh grade, and in this

area, at least, that was still middle school. Sixth through eighth went to one school, and then ninth would be in high school.

"I'm not going to know anybody there, and everyone will be friends from when they were kids. I'm going to hate it."

I shook my head, running my hand up and down Alice's back.

"We're surrounded by military bases, and in this district especially, there are students whose parents are in the military. Meaning they'll be just as new as you. In fact, some will even come into school in the middle of the school year. And by then you will be the one who will seem local."

"I'll never be local here. I don't want to know some military kid. I want to know my friends."

And with that, she stomped away, and I watched her go, knowing that everything we did from here on out would be a fight.

Even getting her to go to therapy once a week so far was like pulling teeth. The only way that I had been able to get her to go at all was that I had tricked her into it the first time, and now the therapist was helping me get her there each time. Alice didn't mind. In fact, she had fun with her therapist. I was there through part of it, but then the girls were able to speak

75

their personal thoughts if needed. Cameron didn't speak.

And Alice talked all about her fairy and fay world.

"I'm going to like second grade. Twos are better because they're even." Alice smiled up at me, and I couldn't help but run my thumb down her cheek.

"Your mom loved second grade. I liked third grade more because we had an amazing teacher. But your mom loved even numbers."

"Mommy always said even numbers would be the best years. And next year I'm going to be eight. And Mommy said that would be a fun year because it's a magical year." Alice's eyes welled. "Will it still be magical if she's not here?"

I swallowed that tug of emotion and ran my hand down her back.

"It's going to be magical. And just because your mother isn't here right now, doesn't mean she's not watching you. She's watching you from afar, and she's going to help make sure it's magical. Even if she can't be here. Because you know your mommy wanted to be here more than anything."

And I wanted my sister to be here more than anything.

"Okay," Alice said with a bright smile before she pulled back and grinned. "Can I go play outside?"

I looked through the large glass French doors at the back of the house and nodded. We weren't in a full neighborhood, since the Wilders had bought this land and were slowly making it so renters could live in the homes that Brooks and his team built. I wasn't sure of the logistics of it, but it was an extra form of money, and hence the homes themselves were gorgeous. I lived in a Craftsman home now, with little details in the wood carvings and tile work that took my breath away.

When I pulled myself out of grief and the unending horror that was trying to figure out how to be a mom when I never thought I would be one in the first place, I couldn't help but stare in wonder at the meticulous and caring work that Brooks had put into this place.

A place that he had just handed me the keys to and yelled at me in order to take it.

He hadn't even been there when we had moved in. Instead, he had gone outside Austin to work on the expansion for the Wilders, leaving his family, my friends, to help move me in.

His house next door had lain empty for this past month, and I didn't know if I was grateful or annoyed about that.

No, I had to be grateful.

Because he had given me security I hadn't even

known I'd needed, and he hadn't asked for a single thing in return.

Instead he had given me space, and now I didn't have to wonder how I would feel when I saw him again.

Of course, he could be home at any moment, and there was no going back.

I looked up the stairs to where Cameron lay in her room, Taylor Swift blaring out of the speakers, and went back to the small office that was off the dining and living area.

It had glass doors as well, and the place was sound-proof somehow, so if I had the doors closed, I could focus on work, but if I had them open, I could hear if the girls needed me.

One whole wall was floor-to-ceiling windows, and we had put my old settee in front of it. That had been in storage this whole time, and now it was a perfect reading nook. Behind my desk were custom book-shelves that I knew Brooks had built himself, including staining them and adding little flourishes like a hidden fairy door.

And it just gave me another glimpse into the man himself.

And didn't that scare me.

My favorite Taylor Swift song played even louder,

and I closed my eyes, letting it soothe me as I hoped it was doing to Cameron.

She didn't know that we shared a similar love for that artist. Or the other countless so-called oldies that she played.

She called them oldies—I called them my favorite artists.

But I wouldn't tell her yet. Trying to find common ground with her would just make her even more angry with me.

Knowing I only had a little while before I had to make dinner, I went through the list again of what I would have to buy for the girls. If I couldn't drag Cameron with me, then Ava said she would watch her while I took Alice out. For some reason, Cameron didn't seem to mind being near Ava and Wyatt. Mostly, Wyatt. That made me smile. No, Cameron may hate me and yell at me often, but those Wilder men, even at their most growliest, couldn't help but make a girl swoon.

I didn't think Cameron had a crush per se, but she listened when the Wilder men spoke. So Wyatt and Ava would be able to watch Cameron if I couldn't get her out of the house to go shopping.

And if all else failed, I could get Cameron to stay on the Wilder property that she somewhat liked, even though I knew she lied to me about it. And then I could get work done.

Like I was supposed to be doing right now.

With a sigh, I brought out my sketchbook and got to work.

I ignored emails, knowing I'd have to get to those tonight when the girls were asleep. Eventually I would sleep, but then again, if I did, I would either be thrown into a nightmare of a plane crash, or worse, one where Brooks was the main feature, and I was then thrown into a plane crash.

I shook my head and tried to get back to work. When my alarm sounded forty-five minutes in, I frowned and realized that Alice hadn't checked in.

Music was still going, and I could hear Cameron stomping up there, so I set my work aside and went out to the backyard to search for Alice.

"Alice! I'm going to start up dinner soon. Where are you?"

The fence line was only on part of the property and not on the rest. It was more like a dog run, where the rest was open so you could see the beauty of the Texas landscape. There was a house to the right of us, but it was an elderly couple, and I rarely saw them. To the left of us, of course, was Brooks, and I hadn't seen him since I had moved in.

But Alice wasn't out near the small copse of trees, or the native bushes that I knew that she liked to play near and pretend she was in fairyland.

"Alice! Where are you?" I asked, my heart racing.

I didn't see her outside, so I ran back in, calling her name.

She wasn't in her room and wasn't in any of the other places that she normally would be.

I knocked on Cameron's door, but she didn't answer.

"Cameron. I'm coming inside. I need to find your sister."

"Don't you dare come inside!" Cameron shouted.

The doors for the girls' room didn't have locks for a reason, and I walked right in. Cameron lay on her bed, journal in hand, and she glared at me.

"This is my space," she snapped.

"And I knocked, and you know the rules. I come in after I knock to check on you. For safety. However, where's your sister?"

"You already lost her? Great supervisor you are," she sneered.

I stared at her, knowing I would have to deal with this soon. But first, I needed to find Alice.

Without saying a word, I whirled on my heels and ran down the stairs before going outside again.

"Alice!" I yelled.

"She's over here, Rory," a familiar, deep voice said smoothly, and I froze, my throat going tight.

Oh, no, no, no, no, no. When had he come home?

I turned to the side and realized that Brooks stood there, Alice in his arms, as she wrapped her little arms around his neck, calmly laying her cheek against his shoulder.

The fences themselves had a small gate to connect them, and I figured it was because Brooks owned the places, but it was all I could do not to but my knees finally gave out.

"Alice. You didn't tell me you were going over there."

"But I saw Mr. Wilder. And he looks just like the other Mr. Wilder. And they're really pretty," she mock-whispered.

Tears pricked my eyes for some reason, even as my lips twitched.

"I see," I said, trying to sound steady.

"Okay there, you know it's not good to run out when Rory needs to know where you are," Brooks said smoothly. "You scared her."

"I didn't mean to scare you," Alice said as she wiggled out of his arms. Brooks set her down carefully as she scurried towards me. The gate was already open, and she slammed into my stomach. I wrapped my arms around her, not realizing I was shaking until I let out a deep breath.

"I'm so sorry. Do you still love me?"

This time, tears did fall, and I went to my knees. "I love you so much, baby girl. You scared me. But it's okay that you're sorry. Just don't do it again."

"I promise." Alice turned over her shoulder and looked at Brooks. "I'm sorry too, Mr. Wilder."

"Call me Mr. Brooks. There's enough Wilders out here."

"Okay, Mr. Brooks. But thank you for showing me your backyard. And thank you for the house." Then she wriggled out of my arms just like she had Brooks's and ran into the house.

I knelt there, mud on my knees, my hands still shaking, wondering what the hell I was doing.

Before I could think, Brooks was there, lifting me up as if I weighed nothing.

"What?" I gasped.

"I was going to stop by and let you know I'm home. If you need anything." That rough voice sent shivers down my spine again, and this time, tears pricked for another reason.

"You scared me," I whispered.

"I get that. I'm sorry that I didn't realize in time what she had done. She just wanted to see what I was up to. And I look enough like Wyatt that she wasn't surprised at who I was."

"I guess I need to do better about stranger danger." I shook my head. "I have no idea what I'm doing, Brooks."

I hadn't meant to blurt the words. In fact, of all people, I shouldn't speak them to him.

But in answer, he pulled me into his arms, and I settled my cheek against his chest. The steady beat of his heart calmed me, and I didn't want to think about the whys of that. Instead, he rubbed his hand down my back much as I'd done with Alice.

"I'm sorry."

"You need to stop being nice to me. I don't know what to do with nice, Brooks," I said honestly.

"I'm not nice," he grunted.

"I know that," I said with a soft laugh that didn't hold much humor. "I'm failing."

"You aren't, Rory. Life has a way of kicking you in the balls, and then you can't figure out how to survive. But you're going to. You're stronger than that. Those girls need you, and you're going to be strong for them. And you're not alone."

"Okay," I said, not sure what else to say.

So instead, I just stood there, letting him hold me, even though I knew I was failing.

And for some reason, being in his arms made me think that maybe, just maybe, I wasn't failing all too badly.

CHAPTER FIVE
BROOKS

"It's about time you're back," Wyatt said as he reached around to grip my shoulder. "While you doing most of the heavy lifting over at the new property is good for me, we've missed you around here."

I raised a brow at my brother. "Are you saying that because you actually missed me here on property or the fact that I cook more than you?"

Wyatt put his hand over his chest and staggered back dramatically. "How dare you. I like your presence."

"You like his enchiladas more," Ava teased as she came forward and pushed her husband out of the way. Then she wrapped her arms around my neck and slapped a noisy, wet kiss on my cheek.

Feeling far more lighthearted than I had been in

over a month, I circled my arms around her waist and spun my sister-in-law in the air.

"I do make a good green chili enchilada."

"Yes, you do. I've missed them so. I realized that I can cook, and Wyatt and I do take turns in the kitchen, but I do enjoy it when you're the one who cooks for us." She fluttered her eyelashes as I set her down on the ground. "What do you say? Will you be our third? It would really help things in the chores department."

Elliot, my cousin, burst out laughing next to us. "Oh, please. Please make this happen. First, I wouldn't be the only triad in the family anymore, and it would annoy Wyatt to no end."

"Did you just proposition my brother?" Wyatt asked, a glare on his face.

My lips twitching, I covered my mouth with my hand and pretended to scratch at my week-old beard. I should probably shave, but my beard grew quickly enough that it was now just at the point where it would be soft again. Not that it truly mattered who it was soft for. The only person I had been kissing recently was Rory, and that wasn't truly that recent. Nor would it ever happen again, as I continued to remind myself.

Amara hadn't liked my beard at all. Even when I used oil on it to make it smooth, she hadn't liked the sensation on her skin.

So, I had usually gone with a completely smooth face for her. I hadn't minded, because Amara never asked for much. I swallowed hard, thinking of her final ask of me. Well, she didn't usually ask for much. Asking me to try again, though? That just wasn't going to happen.

When Rory's face popped into my mind at that very instant, I held back a scowl.

There was no reason to be thinking of Rory in that context. Just because we had slept together, didn't mean it would happen again.

As it was, the anniversary of losing Amara and, subsequently, the anniversary of sleeping with Rory had passed in the month that I had been gone. None of my family had mentioned it because they knew me well enough to even go down that path.

The first anniversary that I had spent with my family, each of them had tried to say something, though there was nothing to say. Then, they'd walked away from that and done their best just to be family.

As Wyatt and Elliot began to squabble, I took a step back and stared at my family, wondering exactly how I'd ended up here.

"I don't actually want to marry him, you jerk. But I do want that enchilada recipe."

"It's yours. And I'll even make them for you sometime. But I'm not marrying you. Sorry. I already did that marriage thing, not doing it again."

People gave me odd looks, and I shrugged, not wanting to get into it. I was a widower. I had been for years now. It wasn't as if grief just left. Yes, I missed my wife. But I didn't think of myself as married any longer. It had been enough years that it wasn't as if I woke up and thought she would be by my side every day. That no longer happened. Sometimes, she'd still be in my dreams, and it would be a daily thing in which we were cooking dinner, perhaps trying to figure out what to go on the grocery list. And she would just be there.

As if no time had passed, and then the guilt would hit. Guilt that I had moved on and perhaps forgotten that she'd been alive this whole time during those years.

Brains were funny things when it came to grief. Because I did miss my wife. I would do anything to have Amara back.

But I wasn't the same man I'd been when she died, and I didn't go day by day into my grief, drinking my pain.

I wasn't ready to move on in terms of getting married and following in my family's footsteps.

But I wasn't a sorry excuse for a human being any longer.

The hairs on the back of my neck stood on end, and I turned to see Rory standing there, speaking with Alexis about something. Had she heard me say I would never marry again? I hoped so. It would make things easier, wouldn't it? To lay that out there, even though there was no way that marriage was ever in the cards for us. We had had one night, a few kisses, and a few moments of connection. But now she was my neighbor, a woman trying to raise two kids she didn't know, and she wasn't my future. Wasn't my path.

Someone cleared their throat beside me, and I turned to see Ridge standing there, his face studying me before looking over toward Rory.

"You here to play ball with us?" Ridge asked as he rocked back on his heels.

It was nice to see Ridge so calm, no more of that darkness that had constantly seeped into his waking days. Because when I had been through hell, Ridge had been through his own version. I still couldn't quite believe that he could walk on two feet, let alone get married and want to start a family.

He had way more balls than I did. Because I wasn't about to do that.

Hell, not only were all of my cousins married and starting families but all three of my brothers were married. Wyatt had Faith, Ava's child from her first marriage, who was right smack in the middle of Cameron and Alice's ages. Then there was Gabriel, my rock star of a brother who was not only married and out on tour, but their child Maisie was a year old now. That still surprised me. Because of all the people settling down in our family, between all of the cousins, Gabriel was never it.

I was now the single Wilder, not married, and I was fine with that.

I forced myself not to look over at Rory.

"Brooks?"

I turned towards Ridge and nodded. "I'm in. Flag football, right? No tackling?"

"We're way too fucking old to tackle," my eldest cousin said as Eli came over, Alexis at his side. That meant Rory and Ava were now talking, but this time with a stranger I didn't recognize.

I glared over at the tall man with longish hair, a big beard, and broad shoulders.

He was tall enough that when he spoke to Rory, he had to hover a bit, angling his shoulders downward so he could hear her. The action made him look as if he were in a possessive hold with her, and I didn't like it.

I held back a frown, wondering why the hell jealousy even had a foothold in me, but I didn't care right then.

Because fuck this. Who was that man, and why the hell was he talking to Rory?

"Oh, that's Callum," Ridge said, studying my face. "You know, Gabriel's brother-in-law?"

"Oh," I remembered now. I'd seen the man here before, and come to think of it, he had been flirting with Rory then, too. Well, fuck this guy.

"Gabriel isn't here, why is he?"

"Remember? He and I are going to go to a few of those local breweries and distilleries to do some cross-promotion and work on some ideas? He owns that small microbrewery up in Colorado." Wyatt studied my face, a frown etching his. "You okay?"

I shook off whatever the hell I was feeling, "Oh, I thought he would be here to visit Maisie."

"Gabriel and Maisie will be here by the end of the week, so it all works out," Ridge said pointedly. "Are you okay, bro?"

"I'm fine. Just wondering why he was here if his sister wasn't. Not my business. I guess we're going to go play ball now?"

"I guess we are," Wyatt said, drawing out the words.

I flipped him off, grateful the kids weren't here. In fact, all of them, including Cameron and Alice, were with some of the other Wilders, having a kids' play day.

More power to all of them for dealing with Cameron. While I knew the girl was breaking inside, and most likely a former ghost of herself, I could hear her screaming at Rory constantly. It took all within me not to rush over to the house next door and try to fix whatever the hell was going on.

Nobody deserved to be yelled at the way Rory was. Cameron had so much spite in her, but I knew it was all because of hurt.

But Rory was hurting right along with her. As was Alice. But that little tyke was freaking adorable. She had walked right up to me and asked if I was a Wilder because I apparently had the look of them, in her words. And I had indeed needed to explain the concept of stranger danger before I had carried her back over to Rory.

Even though the kid was seven years old, she had been small enough to practically fit solidly on my hip, as if she had always been there.

I had always wanted kids. It had been in the plans for me and Amara. But then she hadn't been able to get pregnant right away, and when we'd finally figured out why, it had been too late.

Now that path was never going to be mine, and I understood it.

I wasn't going to be a father like the rest of my

family was on the verge of becoming. Then again, Rory hadn't been a mother up until a month ago. And now she was an aunt, trying to figure out how to deal with one screaming child and one who looked on the verge of breaking down because she was trying to be so calm and collected.

Or maybe I was just looking too far into it.

I shook off the odd feeling as a few of my crew members, both from the current job sites and the expansion, joined in. Not all of the Wilder men were playing because indeed we were getting older. And even though it was flag football, we were probably going to end up tackling each other. It's what we did.

Kendall, my cousin-in-law, came over and grinned, "Am I allowed to play?" she asked.

"Hell no," Evan, her husband, said as he smacked her ass before kissing her hard on the mouth. "You can tackle me later."

Kendall rolled her eyes. "I brought food because apparently that's all I'm good for."

"You know you're good for more," he grumbled against her mouth, and I rolled my eyes.

"Seriously? In front of the family?" I growled.

"Go get you some, and stop judging," Evan snapped, even though his eyes were filled with laughter.

"Be nice. And I don't actually want to play because you guys get all sweaty, and it's gross."

"You like it when I'm sweaty," Evan teased.

And then he leaned down and kissed his wife so softly that I knew that Kendall's knees probably went weak.

It was an odd thing to see because I didn't want to be jealous of it. Not of Kendall, but of that sense of home.

Evan and Kendall had been through their own twists and turns in their relationship, and their lives hadn't been easy. But they had gotten their second chance with each other.

"Be careful, please." Then Kendall moved back and glared at all of us. "No tackling my husband. You're welcome to hurt each other, but if my husband ends up with a bruise, there's going to be poison in your food, and you're not going to know when. And I don't mess with food unless I have to."

Considering she owned two restaurants and was becoming world-renowned for it, I wasn't going to risk anything. And I didn't blame her for that warning. Evan had lost his leg overseas when he had been on active duty, and while he moved around easily now with his prosthetic, I wasn't about to be the one who tackled my cousin and hurt him.

"Insurance doesn't cover the whole prosthetic anyway, so let's not fuck around and find out," Evan said as he pointed at all of us.

"Don't worry. I'm more scared of Kendall than I am of you and insurance companies," Elliot said with a smile.

I shook my head as everybody took teams, and I found myself playing tight end against Callum and Eli's team.

An odd little grin slid over my face as I realized that Callum and I would be the ones running against each other for most of the day since we didn't really have a full defense.

It was our version of flag football, and maybe I'd be able to show this pretty boy exactly what it meant to be on Wilder land.

Not that I was showing off to anyone or anything. That wasn't what today was about.

Trace, Elliot's husband, whistled and was going to play referee. He'd had to deal with a trespasser earlier and had fallen off a roof. Just a first floor, but he was bruised enough and in trouble with both of his spouses, so he wasn't allowed to play today.

I was just glad that Ridge and Trace ran security for the company, and I didn't have to deal with that, especially with the clientele we hosted. We all liked our privacy.

By the second play, I caught the ball and made my way towards the end zone. But that asshole Callum took my flag before I could get there.

I scowled at him as he just grinned, even though the smile didn't quite look right on his face. He was too jagged, too stoic for that grin. But then he went over to the water table and spoke with Rory during a timeout.

I glared at him as Rory tipped her head back and laughed.

I froze, knowing I hadn't heard that laugh in too long. First, because it had been the month from hell, and then because she rarely laughed around me. She usually only did when she didn't realize I was around.

We'd purposely stayed out of each other's way because the connection, the chemistry between us was too enticing to ignore.

And now she was my neighbor.

Because I was the one who had stepped in it.

I shook everything off and went back to the game.

With the next play, Callum got me again, and I cursed under my breath as he whistled a small tune.

The others cheered, and I narrowed my eyes at Rory, who seemed to be on Callum's side.

Well, fuck that.

When it was Callum's turn, I got his flag, but he somehow wheedled out of my hold during the next play, and when they scored a touchdown, the other team cheered, and I ignored my team's need to pretend I hadn't fucked up.

The gloves were off now.

By the third quarter, everybody was sweaty because it was Texas in the summer, so we were shirtless, maybe a little bruised and scraped because now there were only a couple of tackles in, and Callum was going to get the ball. I knew it.

Eli threw, and Callum caught the perfect spiral.

I could have reached for his flag. Yes. I could have.

But Callum caught the ball and winked over at Rory.

And I didn't even realize what had happened.

I tackled Callum to the ground, slamming him into the Texas clay. He let out a grunt but kept the ball. When Trace whistled, I tried to stand up, but Callum gripped my shoulder.

"Something you're worried about?" the man asked, his voice low, sarcasm dripping.

"Fuck off," I growled. I had no right to be this angry, no right to be this possessive.

But here I was.

"You better do something about it then, shouldn't you?"

"Fuck. Off," I repeated.

"If you don't get off me right now, I'm going to have to punch you, and it's going to be a thing. And I don't think the little mouse you're looking at is going to really like you getting your ass beat."

I shoved up, pushing him deeper into the dirt, before I walked off, doing my best not to look at Rory.

However, I couldn't help but meet her gaze.

Her eyes were wide, her lips parted, and the small flush riding her cheekbones went straight to my cock.

That damn heat.

No amount of walking away and pretending it wasn't there worked. Because I wanted her. I had wanted her from that first kiss. But I wasn't about to do anything about it. Not when it came to Rory.

Not when it came to the one woman who might just make me keep the promise I had made to my dead wife.

CHAPTER SIX
RORY

I knew it was hot in Texas. That was sort of the whole thing about the state. And South Texas was hot, humid, and sticky.

And yet I knew I was all three of those things and it had nothing to do with the fact that it was summer outside of San Antonio, Texas, and everything to do with the now shirtless, so-called flag football game in front of me.

"Darling, I think you need this," Ava said from beside me as she handed me a cup of icy water. I chugged half of it without even looking at her and forced myself to pull my gaze from the tableau in front of me.

"Do they do this often?" I asked, my voice going slightly high-pitched.

Ava's lips twitched before she turned back to the sight in front of us.

"Not often enough." She shook her head before cupping her hands in front of her mouth.

"Go Wyatt! That's it, baby! Pound those guys into the ground!"

Wyatt rolled his eyes at his wife. "Babe. These are my brothers and cousins. Maybe use a different word?" he drawled, and my lips twitched.

"Yes, maybe don't use the word pound."

I shifted slightly on the outdoor chair that I had borrowed from somebody, my cutoffs feeling far too confining. Every time I moved, my thighs pressed together, my clit rubbing, all because of the shirtless man in front of me.

I pulled an ice cube out of the plastic glass of water and slowly began to run it over my collarbone and chest, needing to cool down.

At that moment, however, Brooks turned to me, his gaze following each movement. I swallowed hard before my tongue darted out, swiping over my lips.

I watched as a bead of sweat slid down his chest, over his pecs, down through his rock-hard abs, and the tiny trail of hair that went down below his gym shorts.

I took another gulp of water, telling myself to calm down.

Just because it was a bunch of sweaty, naked men sliding against one another while playing with balls, didn't mean that this was my version of a nightmare.

Or a wet dream.

Why was it so hot in Texas?

Brooks gave me a look that I didn't want to interpret before going back to the game.

"So, you want to tell me exactly what is going on between you and my brother-in-law?" Ava asked, and I drained my glass.

"Nothing. It's just hot out here."

"I'm pretty sure the heat went from 95 degrees to at least 200 with the look that you two shared."

I raised a brow at her. "I don't know what you're talking about. It's just Brooks. And apparently it's been a while for me since I've been so busy. It just got a little overheated. Plus, I'm worried that I haven't heard from the girls in the past twenty minutes."

I checked my phone again for a text from them or Alexis, but nothing. I was a terrible aunt. The first chance where I'd been able to take a breath and a moment by myself, I'd run. The girls had started school, and while things were going well, as in they weren't talking to me about it, and their therapist was hopeful. Yet it didn't feel like enough. Because when the girls had been invited to spend the night with Alexis and the others as part of a party planning practice, I'd jumped at the chance.

Yet, really, I'd only done so because Alice had looked so excited, and Cameron had only rolled her eyes once. That had to count for progress.

Or perhaps I was a terrible aunt turned guardian.

Ava gave me her glass of water, taking mine from me. "Drink that. And maybe I'll get you drunk on wine later."

I pressed my lips together, worry once again winning out over whatever feeling I'd had while watching Brooks... well, do anything. "Are you sure that we should be having a girls' night? I know that Alexis and the others said that it was okay that Cameron and Alice spent the night at their place so the girls could have a different environment for the evening, but I feel like I'm abandoning them."

The Wilder women had girls' nights at least once a month. Before everybody had started to have children, it had been more often, especially because they had all lived on the property, and they literally owned a winery. In fact, one of Ava's cousins-in-law was the actual winery expert and always had a vast selection of different wines for us to try. Not to mention that Kendall was now a world-renowned chef, so there was always something yummy to eat.

Over time, the dinners had slowed down to just once a month, if they couldn't get any more time in, but they put in the effort to make it work.

I had been invited a few times, or rather, I was invited every time that Ava went, but I didn't always make it. Sometimes, I was on deadline, and frankly, sometimes, being on the property at the same time as Brooks was a little too much for me.

But considering I was sitting here in the heat surrounded by his family and friends and watching him play football all sweaty-like, maybe I was a lost cause.

Again, though, it wasn't as if my brain could make this work. Everything was already too much when it came to my life. Yes, having him hold me and telling me that I could do this and that I wasn't alone was nice, but in the end, that couldn't mean anything.

Brooks wanted nothing to do with me or hadn't before this, and we had been circling each other for far too long to even think about what it could mean.

So no, I wasn't going to let myself want more.

Especially because Alice and Cameron had to be my first priority.

And Cameron hated me, so it wasn't as if I was gaining any headway there.

"You know that the girls wanted to spend the night and have a girl-time sleepover. Alice is a little spider monkey that will cling to anyone in our family because she's so adorable, and I know she needs that touch. Cameron?" Ava shrugged before she leaned down and pulled out a soda from the cooler at her feet. "Cameron will come around."

"You say that, and yet I don't quite believe it. She hates me."

"She doesn't. She's just hurting." Ava paused before flipping the tab on the can. "She's grieving, but are you?"

I frowned as I stared at my friend. "Of course I am. But the girls are more important."

"They are important, but so are you. You need to take care of yourself." And she gave a pointed look towards the men on the field, and I glared at her.

"Taking care of myself does not mean letting one of them help me with it."

"Well, since most of them are married, I don't think it's just one of them."

"Ava."

"What about Callum? He's been giving you looks. And I saw the way that you two hit it off last time he was here."

I turned and looked at Callum Ashford, the man that I had indeed clicked with quite well when he had first come to visit his new niece over a year ago.

However, it hadn't been that type of clicking. Instead, he had just been easy to talk to. Maybe there could have been a spark, but my heart had been going in a different direction, even though I had yelled at it for doing so. And from the way that Callum pointedly didn't talk about a certain someone in his life, I had a feeling so did his.

Yet, every time he looked at me, he winked or brushed my hair from my face or gently ran his finger down my upper arm.

However, I knew he was just screwing with Brooks.

But why?

"I don't have time to think about men. Or anything like that. And I am grieving, Ava. My sister's gone, and I hate it. But I have to focus on the girls. Who I've abandoned today so they can hang out with people who aren't me. And because everybody thought I could use a break." I ran my hands over my face. "I have no idea what I'm doing with my nieces. Every single day I feel like I'm learning something new and just trying not to fail."

Ava reached out and gripped my hand. "You're not failing. You're in a situation that doesn't have any answers. You are so strong, my friend. And I hate the fact that you're going through this. But you're not alone. We're all here. You know that, right?"

Tears pricked my eyes, and I swallowed hard, leaning over to rest my head on Ava's shoulder. "I know. And I know I could never imagine what my life would be without you. Thanks for everything."

"Now, drink this other glass of water, and go stare at some half-naked men. Because we don't need to be melancholy right now. We could be melancholy later and in perpetuality."

My lips twitched, but I knew she was right. It was time to focus on the quiet moments because nothing truly felt quiet or sane anymore.

I quickly drank another sip of my water before standing up with the others and cheering on the game in front of me.

While it was technically flag football, some of the guys slammed into each other for fun.

I did my best to keep my gaze off of Brooks, however, because the more I stared at him, the more I was afraid others would notice.

Because nothing good could come from me wanting Brooks.

He clearly didn't want me, and I didn't have time to want him.

And that was the same thing, right?

Or, at least, close enough.

Callum came over after a moment and lifted his chin at me. "Hey. Having fun?"

I looked down and studied him, my gaze traveling over his very nice set of abs and the way that he looked like he could have been molded from clay or something much harder, but yet, there was no zing. It wasn't like it was with Brooks. And that was a problem.

"I'm just glad you guys aren't hurting each other. Though, you do look a little hot." He raised a brow at that, and I rolled my eyes before handing him a water. "Go have fun out there. Don't break anything."

"No promises, baby girl," he called out, and my cheeks blushed as a few people I didn't know wolf-whistled at that.

"Baby girl?" Ava mouthed.

"Shush," I whispered.

"I have so many questions right now," Aurora whispered as she came to my other side. "Like, when did that start?"

I bumped my hip against hers. "It's not. He's just screwing with me."

Or rather, he was screwing with Brooks. But I wasn't about to say that out loud.

"He wants to be screwing something," Ava muttered, and I choked on my water before glaring at her.

Heat scorched my skin, and it had nothing to do with the sun. I looked up to see Brooks studying my face.

I swallowed hard and did my best to pull my gaze from him as the whistle sounded.

Somebody called out a number and then a name, but it was all I could do not to stare at Brooks as his body moved in such quick motions. He worked with his hands for a living, and I knew exactly what those hands felt like on my skin. But the way that he moved with such grace and strength? It just did something to me. I barely resisted the urge to press my thighs together again.

Then Callum whistled at me, and I looked up, only to see Brooks slam the other man into the ground.

"Brooks!" I called out, my voice sharp.

"Oh, that's going to leave a bruise," Aurora called out.

The two of them were growling at each other as I ran over, not thinking. I put my hand on Brooks's shoulder and pulled him back.

"Seriously? It's not a full contact sport."

"Well, Brooks and I just had to say a few things to each other. Help me up, baby?" Callum asked, holding out his hand.

I glared at him, wondering what the hell he was up

to before I pulled him up to his feet, my back pressing against Brooks' front.

I swallowed hard, ignoring the heat of both men. They were both above six feet and towered over me, and suddenly, I felt like a little mouse with two giant lions growling at me.

I cleared my throat before shaking my head at the two of them and walking back to Ava.

I had no idea what that was about, but I wanted nothing to do with it.

Or at least that's what I kept telling myself.

"I have so many questions," Ava said after a moment, and I rolled my eyes.

"And I don't have any answers. It's pottery and wine tonight, right?" I asked.

"Yes. And we should go head to that now," Aurora answered. "The boys can keep getting all sweaty together."

My lips twitched, but I didn't turn back to see if Brooks or Callum were looking over.

I didn't want Callum, and I knew he didn't want me. But he was annoying Brooks for some reason. How was I supposed to tell him it was all in vain?

Because Brooks didn't want me, and I couldn't want him.

Reminding myself of that, I pulled out my phone.

ME

Everything going okay?

CAMERON

Fine.

I sighed, knowing that I had given her a phone so we could keep in contact for emergencies and just so I knew where she was, but she hated texting me back.

But the rule was, if she wanted to keep the phone, she had to answer me.

One-word answers, though, were all I was going to get out of her.

Instead of belaying the point, I pressed her contact information and called.

"I said I was fine," Cameron snapped.

I closed my eyes and prayed for patience. "Cameron, tone. And I know you're okay, but I also wanted to talk to Alice."

"Fine," Cameron grumbled.

I sighed, knowing I was going to have to work on her attitude. I just had no idea where to start. Brooks had helped for an instant, and Cameron had at least apologized for talking back to me in the way she had, but every time that I tried to discipline her, I saw my sister's face.

And felt the emptiness that was losing my twin.

Tears pricked my eyes as I followed my friends towards the main Wilder building for our evening in, as Alice came on the line.

"Hi, Aunt Rory. I am about to play with Faith. We have a book stamper."

I smiled softly. "The one for the edges? What color are you choosing?"

"Pink, of course. And roses. I'm really excited. Do you think we can paint some of your books? The ones that you drew for?"

"We can make that happen. You have fun tonight with Cameron and the others, and tomorrow when you get back, we can look through some of the books I have drawings in." *At least the ones that were safe for work,* I thought to myself. "What do you say?"

"I love it! And maybe you can help me figure out how to draw a flower of my own?"

"I can do that, baby," I whispered, my heart swelling.

Because Alice was trying. She was so lost, so scared, and just wanted to be with everybody at all times.

And I had no idea what the hell I was doing with either one of them.

"I have to go now. I love you," Alice whispered.

"I love you too," I said, a single tear sliding down my cheek.

I swallowed hard as the phone clicked off, knowing Cameron wasn't going to even try to get back on.

I was failing both of them in subtle ways, but I was at least trying.

At least, that's what I kept telling myself.

"Faith says they're having fun," Ava said softly as she wrapped her arm around my shoulder.

"Yeah, Alice says so too."

"Nothing from Cameron?" Aurora asked, her voice low.

I shook my head. "No. But at least she answered her phone?"

"Yes, there is that," Aurora said gently as she squeezed my hand.

"You know what? I could really use a drink. Just lean into this whole girls' night thing," I said after a moment.

"Good thing we happen to have drinks here," Maddie said as the Wilder woman came forward and gestured towards the large array of wine, cheeses, and fine foods on the table.

"We have snacks, a few wines I want you to try out, and then, pottery."

"It's just painting tonight," Aurora added. "I figured we could at least try to work out glazes and paints for the kiln before we invest in pottery wheels or even slabs," she said with a laugh.

"The only reason I know any of the words you're saying is because I watched The Great Pottery Throw Down," I said after a moment. "And I don't know much."

"You know more than I do," Ava put in. "But you know, you are the artist of us all. So I can't wait to see what you're painting turns out to be."

I rolled my eyes. "I don't paint on vases or teapots. And if I'm drinking, it's not going to be too pretty."

Maddie handed me a glass of red and grinned.

"This is a pinot noir, and you're going to love it. And not just because I say so. And I want to hear all about your work. I've only seen some of it, but Ava here tells me you have not safe for work art? As in, the scenes from the books that I love? Tell me everything."

I looked around the room at the Wilder women who'd joined us and a few friends of theirs and let out a breath.

I had been alone for so long because it was easier to do so, and I reminded myself that my sister had left, but now she was gone forever.

And I was out of my depth.

But with these women, maybe it wasn't so bad.

Maybe I could figure something out.

So I sipped the wine that was indeed amazing and took a seat in front of a teapot.

"Well, I can't talk about too much of the work I'm doing, except for one of them does have a dragon."

"As in a dragon that the heroine rides? Or that the heroine *rides*?" Ava asked.

"Why not both?" Aurora said before she put her hand over her mouth. "I can't believe I just said that out loud."

Considering Aurora was sweet, and I thought innocent, I burst out laughing, shaking my head.

"It's the former, but I have drawn something of the latter. This one, though, the hero and heroine are on top of a dragon."

"I want to know everything, and I need to know the book," Maddie said as she pointed at me.

"Now, let's get to glazing, and tell me so we can add to my TBR."

Laughing, I took a seat, knowing that I really wasn't okay. Yes, I could laugh, I could smile, but something needed to change. Only I had no idea what it was going to be.

I continued to drink, ignoring the fact that I was probably having a little too much. But it wasn't as if I was driving anywhere. I had a place to stay for the night, and then I would pick up the girls and figure out the next phase of this new life of mine.

And I was not going to think about Brooks or Callum. Because Callum was only flirting with me to annoy Brooks.

And Brooks wanted nothing to do with me.

I was the one who had been sitting on the sidelines, practically having an orgasm, just watching Brooks take off his shirt.

I was the lost cause and had been ever since that night in the airport.

By the time I finished my teapot and was helping the others with their different art pieces, I was feeling warm and happy and only partially drunk.

Not too drunk that I was going to make terrible decisions, but enough that maybe all of my worries weren't so hard on my chest.

Or at least that's what I wanted to tell myself.

"Knock, knock," a deep voice said from behind us, and I watched as Elijah walked into the room, eyes only for his wife.

Maddie looked up at him, smiling wide.

"You're early."

He shook his head. "No, you guys are running late. You said you wanted me to pick you up by 8:00, so we could have the rest of the night. Is that okay?"

I looked down at my phone, surprised. "Oh, it's late," I blurted.

"Just a little," Elijah said simply before he leaned down and brushed his lips against Maddie's.

My heart swelled, and a little jealousy slid in.

I shouldn't be jealous. It wasn't as if I'd ever been in a serious relationship like that. Had ever been wanted the way that Maddie clearly was.

And when everyone else's significant others began to trickle in, taking their women home. The loneliness that settled in felt far starker than usual.

Prepared to walk myself to my little gray cabin, I pulled out my phone, knowing that the girls had texted good night earlier while I had done the same, but no other emergency texts had come in.

Nobody needed me, and I was alone. But that's what I was good at. Right?

"Rory," a deep voice said behind me, and I whirled, nearly tilting over. Brooks reached out and gripped my elbows, keeping me steady.

"What are you doing here?" I blurted, the hairs on the back of my neck standing on end.

Wyatt had already carried Ava out, except she didn't drink often and had nuzzled into his neck. Everyone else was trickling out, having said their goodbyes, and now I was here, alone with Brooks. Or at least practically.

"I wanted to make sure you got to the cabin okay. You're staying in the little cottage, right?"

I nodded, letting out a breath. "Yes. But I'm fine. You don't have to worry about me."

"Rory, we both know that's not true."

My heart kicked, and I had no idea what he meant by that. "I'm fine. You should go do what you were planning on doing. I'll make it back on my own."

"I'm not letting you walk around with alcohol in your system alone."

"I'm safe here. You know that, right?"

"Maybe, but I'm still not doing it."

I met his gaze, annoyed because I had no idea what the hell he was thinking. But that was the problem with Brooks Wilder. I never knew what he was thinking.

Instead, I grabbed my bag and walked with him out into the heated night. Even though I only wore a T-shirt and cut-off shorts, it was still warm enough that I couldn't feel a nighttime chill. Which probably was an issue that I needed to worry about, or maybe it was the heat from being beside Brooks.

It was a short walk to the cabin. A small gray one that I knew had special significance in the Wilder family. Though I didn't know every story that came with it.

I unlocked the door, ready to turn and say goodbye to Brooks, but there he was, standing behind me. He had put his shirt back on, as well as a pair of jeans, but the ball cap that he usually wore was gone. He just stared at me, confusion in his gaze.

"Thank you. Though you didn't need to do that."

"But I did." He reached out then and ran his thumb along my jawline.

I swallowed hard, heat and hate sliding through me.

But the hate wasn't for him.

No, that was the problem. It was never for him.

"Sleep with me," I blurted, and I wasn't even aware I was going to say the words until they were out.

"You're drunk, Rory."

I shook my head, feeling far more sober than I had before.

"I'm not. And I don't mean fuck me. Just sleep with me. I could really use a hug. And I know that's desperate, but I don't care. Just hold me? For a bit?" I let out a breath. "Because I have a feeling you need one too."

He stared at me then, and I had to wonder who exactly had just said all those words. Because they sure as hell didn't sound like me.

Instead, he ran his thumb over my lips before letting out a breath.

"Okay. Okay."

And without another word, he closed the door behind him, locking it. And then he followed me into the bedroom as we toed off our shoes, and not even bothering to take off my makeup or my clothes, I slid under the covers as he did the same. His jeans were warm against my legs, and I snuggled into him, needing that warmth.

I hated the fact that his arms felt like home, even though he was nothing of the sort.

But as he finally let out a breath, his heart beating softly against my ear, I sank into him, letting myself pretend.

Pretend that I knew what I was doing. Pretending that I wasn't failing my family.

And pretending I could be someone that Brooks Wilder could want.

That Brooks Wilder could love.

And I fell asleep letting the facade wash over me, knowing that it would end with the next breath, and it would be something I would just have to get over.

Again.

CHAPTER SEVEN
BROOKS

I'd left before she'd woken up. Frankly, I shouldn't have stayed at all. Yet the feeling of Rory in my arms continued to slide into my memory as if she'd never left. I'm not sure why I agreed to sleep next to her, but I hadn't been able to say no. It was just as if it were a normal thing—to sleep next to the woman who wasn't mine.

I didn't know what we had between us, though I knew it had to be nothing. Because no good could come from a relationship.

I nearly tripped over my own feet at the thought of a relationship.

Because there was no way I'd be having a relationship with that woman.

In the two weeks since ladies' night and the football game, I had done my best to avoid her.

Which was pretty hard to do, considering we were now neighbors.

I might be her landlord, there to help her with anything around the house, but she hadn't asked for help yet, and from what Ava had mentioned in passing, she hadn't needed it.

And it wasn't as if I was going to allow Rory to pay rent. No, she didn't get to pay rent when she was having to feed two more mouths. I might not have children, but I knew they came with a shit ton of needs. Between clothes, food, school, activities, and just life in general, kids were expensive. And I wasn't sure what Rory made with her job. It wasn't a nine-to-five job that I understood.

Not that my job was nine-to-five.

I pulled off my hat, running my hands through my hair as I folded the brim a bit. I had completely ruined my previous hat, the one that I had worn-in over the years. Now, I was trying to force a UT ball cap into some form of work attire that didn't look as if it had just come off the shelf.

"What are you thinking about?" East asked, and I looked over at my cousin, who'd come up to my side when I hadn't been paying attention.

East was the so-called handyman of The Wilder Bunch. He was so much more than that. Before I had come along, he had been the one who had done most of the construction and upkeep for the entire resort. The only thing he really didn't take care of was the winery itself because we had an entire staff who were trained and brilliant at that.

I wasn't sure how East had handled the resort, all of the cabins, the barn for events, and countless other outbuildings by himself or with his small team when he had finally begun to hire them.

Now we worked together when I wasn't contracting on other businesses and homes around the area.

I liked East. Yes, he was an asshole, but sometimes I could be too.

I thought about how I had been treating Rory recently and realized that maybe it was more than just sometimes.

"I'm just trying to get my hat to work. It's too stiff."

"You do realize if it was any other Wilder next to you, there would've been a joke with that," East drawled.

I snorted at the other man as I noticed we had pretty much the same attire. Worn jeans, work boots that yielded more towards cowboy boots than anything, and, of course, a ball cap. East had the Air

Force logo on his, while I was apparently ready to hook on horns.

"When are you heading back to Austin?" East asked after a moment as we walked towards our project site next to the spa on our property.

"In a couple of weeks." I ran my hand along the back of my neck.

"My team has it all handled, and although Eli is working hard on all the permits for everything, paperwork takes time. We have what we need to get this far, and now we're just in the next set of zones that take more inspections and everything. I'll head out tomorrow to check it out, but I won't be working on it for a few weeks. So you got me here for a while."

"Well, considering we're working on an expansion out here, and I know you have a few homes that you want to build, you've been a little busy."

There was something in his tone that sounded a bit off, and I frowned.

"Is there something you want to say?"

East let out a breath. "Lark wanted me to quiz you to see how you're doing and what's going on with you and Rory."

I paused, looking at the man before throwing my head back and laughing. Others on my team and a few passers-by who had to be guests looked over at us but continued on with what they were doing.

"I don't know why you find that funny," East said as my laughter finally died down.

"Every other person in our family would have tried to wheedle their way down that subject a little bit easier. They would have pretended that they weren't trying to care about my well-being or whatever the hell you think it is. You just came right out and said it."

"I'll have you know I was trying to be circumspect while asking about work things before. I'm just not good at this shit."

"No, you're not. Although, I'm not very good at it either."

"I don't know... you wheedled information out of Gabriel more than the rest of us."

We each picked up our tools and got to work, the feeling of doing something with my hands that could produce anything settling me down.

"Gabriel's always been easy to talk to for me. Ridge was the one who kept things quieter than the rest of them. Wyatt acts as if he is boisterous and doesn't have any secrets, and you have to dig deep beneath the humor to find them. Ridge closes up and acts as if the world can't hurt him even though he's dying inside. Or at least he was. Gabriel? You just need to sit next to him for a little bit longer, and he will finally break because he puts it in his songs more often than not."

East studied my face before nodding slowly. "It's funny how the four of you are so different, and you guys have spent more time together as adults than we have."

That much was true. Although my brothers and I hadn't lived near each other for a few years, we were able to spend more time together as a group because there were fewer of us.

The seven other Wilders, though, had a harder time because there were so many.

When my aunt and uncle had died, things had become even harder for them as a group. Eliza had moved up to Colorado with her first husband, and now was happily married and raising two kids with her second husband. With that one treating her the way she should have been treated all along. The other cousins had each joined the military, and finding time and leave in order to make a family reunion happen just didn't happen. But now since we all lived nearby, something that still surprised me, we could have a family reunion minus our parents anytime. And I knew my parents were going to visit soon. They wanted to see their grandbabies, especially since Gabriel and Briar were back in town for a few weeks.

Of course my hand fisted at that thought because

that meant although Callum had gone home to check on his brewery and the other siblings, he was back in town to visit his sister.

I knew there was something rumbling under the surface with that man, not with Rory, though. At least, I didn't think so. He was just egging me on, not that I should be able to allow that to happen. Because nothing was going to happen with Rory.

But Callum was visiting Briar more often than not because of something with that family, but it wasn't any of my business. And, like I had just been saying to East, if something was wrong with Gabriel, he'd let us know in his own time, and I wouldn't have to wedge it out.

"Now that we've discussed the rest of your siblings, would you like to just answer the question so I can let the others know? Because I'm pretty sure the women are going to corner Rory soon."

I froze in the act of bending over to lift a box, before I straightened and frowned. "What do you mean corner Rory?" I asked, the protectiveness in my tone surprising me.

"We all saw you walk her home, at least to the cabin, and not leave until morning. We might not be a small town, but the Wilder property acts like it. You know that."

I cursed under my breath. "And you guys didn't think to talk about it with me in the past two weeks? You think we're sneaking around or something?"

We were, or at least we had been. No, that wasn't right. It wasn't sneaking; it just wasn't happening.

And that circular reasoning was confusing me.

"I don't know what the hell's going on, but maybe you should think about it."

"What's there to think about? I'm not dating anyone. I don't plan on it."

"Is that what Amara would've wanted?" East asked, and I staggered back, wondering why this Wilder of all Wilders would be the one to finally reach that wall that I had put between us for so long.

"I don't want to talk about Amara."

"Maybe that's the problem."

"East. I loved my wife. I grieve because I'm always going to, but I'm not in a deep state of mourning where I can't get up. I don't want to date because I already did it."

"So you're just going to be alone forever. Going to die a born-again virgin?"

"I didn't say I wasn't going to have sex again."

"So you're going to go from a love of your life to meaningless sex. That makes total sense."

"I'm done talking about this," I growled.

"Fine, I'll leave you with this. Tonight is Singles' Night down at the retreat. It's make your own pizza because, apparently, Elliot is in the mood to add random themes to his plans. I know Ava is going to force Rory to go because the girls have been doing well in their new school, and therefore, they get a night out with Ava. Or at least that's what Ava's framing it as."

"Is there a reason you're telling me this?" I bit out.

"Fine, I'll put it plainly. Rory is going to be at a Singles' Night, and a certain Ashford is going to be there as well because of his own reasons. Briar just mentioned it."

I cursed under my breath. "Why does it matter that Callum and Rory are going to be at a Singles' Night together?" I asked, the bitterness on my tongue practically stinging.

"I don't know, Brooks, why does it matter?" East asked before the traitor went back to work, whistling under his breath as if he hadn't just shoved a stick in the hornet's nest that was my brain.

"So, you either got roped into this, or you're finally going to make a move," my arch nemesis, who shouldn't have been my arch nemesis, said, and I glared at Callum.

"I'm just here because the women made me," I lied. Although it might not quite be a lie now that I thought about it.

"Okay, buddy. And you keep telling yourself that."

"Is there a reason you are here?" I finally asked, annoyed at the other man. Because in any other instance, I thought maybe the guy and I could be friends. He was just as much of an asshole as I could be. But there was just something about him, like how he looked at Rory as she walked over to us. She had on knee-high soft tan boots, and a red dress that went to right above her knees and had three-quarter length sleeves. The long V between her breasts showed slight cleavage every time she moved, and I couldn't help but let out a shaky breath every time I looked at her.

"Hey Rory, you want to be my pizza buddy?" the man drawled, his voice deep and scratchy.

Rory looked between us, eyes wide. "You guys were forced into this too?" she asked, her voice soft.

"Yes," we both said at the same time, and I growled at Callum before looking over at Rory.

"The girls have a good day at school?" I asked, the words coming quickly.

Her shoulders dropped slightly, and I frowned.

"They did. I think. Alice tells me every single thing about it, and we go over her homework, and it's fun. At least, I think it's fun, but then I have no idea what Cameron is doing. I force her to let me look at her homework, just so I know she's doing it, but she doesn't say a word."

"I know she's talking with Ava a bit," I whispered. Because I was studying her face so intently, I saw the flinch. I hated that I was once again the cause.

"I know, and I'm grateful for that. Because at least she's saying something to someone. But we are three weeks into the school year, and I still have no idea what I'm doing."

"You'll figure it out, Rory," Callum put in before I could. "Those are good kids, and you're a good aunt. You've got this."

Rory smiled at him then, and I wanted to push the asshole out of the way.

Why the hell was I getting so territorial over a woman who wasn't mine. I had been very clear that she wasn't and couldn't be mine.

And yet, I couldn't help but remember a promise that I hadn't made, or maybe I had in the end.

Damn it.

I had made that promise. Because she wouldn't have let me leave otherwise.

I didn't want to think about that whisper in my ears.

I opened my mouth to say something, but Rory wasn't paying attention to me. Instead, she and Callum had moved off to the nearest table, pizza dough in front of them. Kendall stood at the front of the room, looking excited about the evening.

Stewing, I went to Rory's other side and forced my way onto the table. "Okay, if we have to do this, at least I'm getting pizza out of the deal."

Rory stiffened for a moment before she smiled up at me. "Let me guess, spicy sausage and hot peppers?"

"That sounds damn good to me," Callum said as he bumped his hip against her.

I glared at the other man over Rory's head as she looked down at the toppings, and Callum just beamed.

The smile didn't reach his eyes, and I knew he was fucking with me. Why the hell was he doing that? But the real question was, why the hell was it working?

"I actually like non-red sauces more than anything."

Rory looked up at me, eyes wide. "Seriously? I love white pizza. And Alfredo pizza. I'm not a huge tomato fan."

I nodded. "Same. Which disgusts the rest of my family."

"It really does," Kendall said as she moved to our side. "Okay, each of you are going to make your own personal pizza, and we're going to have fun."

"If you say so, Kendall," I said, sarcasm dripping over my tone.

My cousin-in-law just beamed. "You're going to love it. And you're going to get an amazing pizza in the end." Kendall patted my cheek before she went to another table.

Holding my gaze from Rory as she began to roll out the dough, I finally looked at the rest of the room.

There had to be thirty people in this kitchen, everybody laughing, speaking to one another as if they knew each other or wanted to get to know each other. I didn't know how many years they had been working on Singles' Nights or if this was the first one, but it turned out to be a hit so far.

At least for the business side. I still didn't know what the hell I was doing here.

"Hey, I think you stole my flour," Callum teased, and Rory rolled her eyes.

"You're starting to sound like the girls if you're going to continue to fight over that," Rory sing-songed.

Annoyed at the way Callum continued to flirt with her, I pulled the dough out of the bowl and used my hands to roll it out into somewhat of a circle.

Rory met my gaze as I looked over at her before her attention went to my hands and the way that my forearms flexed when I moved the dough.

I watched as her throat worked when she swallowed, and I tilted my hips away from her, hiding the fact that just looking at her gave me a hard-on.

What the hell was wrong with me?

I cleared my throat and reached for the white sauce for my pizza. Callum met my gaze over Rory's head again, and he winked before gesturing at her for some reason. I didn't know what the man was up to, and I didn't like it.

Instead, I began to throw cheese and chicken and artichokes haphazardly on the pizza. I was usually a better cook than this, but at this point, I didn't care.

"So you're going for the more is more route?" Rory asked, teasing in her tone.

I looked down at the mess of the pizza that I made and shrugged. "Food is food. And whatever I can't eat, I'll give to you so that way the girls have leftovers."

A smile quirked her lips. "As if you can't eat an entire pizza yourself."

"I can, but I'm a bit older now, and even without tomatoes, the heartburn is going to kick."

"Tell me about it. I don't know how Cameron and

Alice can scarf down as much pizza as they want and not feel sick later. Oh, the joys of youth."

"It's good they have some joys then," I whispered.

Rory smiled at me, and I felt like I did the right fucking thing.

Finally.

"Hey Rory, what do you think, extra pineapple on this pizza?" Callum asked, drawing her attention away and I glared at the other man even as Rory laughed.

"Look at you, creating drama with pineapple."

"I try," the other man drawled.

The other man kept flirting with her, and I wanted to punch that little smirk off his face.

I knew he was just doing it to egg me on, and part of me wanted to pull Rory back and claim her as mine.

Even though that would've been the worst idea.

By the time all of our pizzas were ready to be put in the oven, Kendall and her staff said they would take care of the rest.

"And when it's ready, it's all about the taste testing with the Wilder Wine, of course. If you'd like something a little more hoppy or less alcoholic, we've got that for you too. So don't worry, we've got something for everyone."

Other people begin to mingle as Callum took a phone call out in the hallway.

My dick ached, and I couldn't help but watch as Rory worried her lip with her teeth.

"That's it," I growled, ripping my gaze from her mouth.

"What's it?" she asked, and her eyes widened once again as I took her by her arm and pulled her into an empty office that we rented out to businesses here for retreats.

"What on earth is wrong with you, Brooks?" Rory asked. But she didn't get a chance to ask again because I closed the door behind her, locked it, and then slammed my mouth to hers.

She stiffened for a moment, and I was afraid I had done the wrong thing before she wrapped her arms around my neck and groaned into me.

I pressed her back to the door, kneading that mouth of hers.

"I fucking missed this taste," I whispered, the words tearing from me.

Rory let out a shaky breath against me, not moving her hands away. "Same."

"Can't stop, Rory. Every time I see you, I need to have my hands on you. And I know it's the wrong time. I know we said we shouldn't. But I don't know what the hell's wrong with me."

The last words could have been a slap to either one of us, but instead, she let out a slow breath.

"Me, too. We don't have time for this. And we both said we wouldn't, and yet I can't stop thinking about you. And I know I shouldn't bare myself like that because I'm only asking to be hurt, but I want you. I want this. Whatever this is."

"Just let me have you. I don't know for tonight, or for tomorrow. But just you. I promise. No one else."

She nodded. "No one else."

And then my mouth was on hers again, and my hands were on her ass. I lifted her up, and she wrapped her legs around my waist before I walked us both to the empty desk. I shoved the lamp off the table, ignoring the way the light bulb shattered, and covered her mouth with mine.

"I've missed this," I whispered again as I tugged on her hair. She moaned against me, so I wrapped her long hair around my fist and tugged harder.

"You like that?" I asked, meeting her gaze.

She nodded, swallowing hard. "Yes. Because it's you."

I didn't know how to take that or why either one of us was being so honest after all this time, but instead, I leaned into it and took her mouth again.

"I'm so thankful you are wearing a dress right now,"

I murmured as I slid my hand up her bare thigh. She shuddered in my hold, and I looked at her lower lip before biting down.

"Brooks," she breathed.

"I've got you. I've got you."

And when my hand met the tiniest piece of fabric ever, I groaned.

"Part of me hoped you weren't wearing panties. The rest of me is damn happy you were considering there were other men in that room."

"Possessive, are you?" Rory asked as she ran her hands up and down my chest.

"You haven't seen the half of it."

I took her mouth again before I ran my hand around her thigh and my thumb over her sweet heat.

She shivered in my arms, and I smiled against her.

"Look at you. Your panties are already damp. Is this for me? Is your pussy wet because of me? Tell me the truth."

"Only you. You know that."

"Good." I bit her jaw as she pulled my shirt up so she could run her hands up and down my back, touching skin.

I let out a groan at her touch and let her explore as I slid my thumb over her cotton-covered slit.

"Do you want my mouth or my cock. How do you

want to come, baby?" I asked, my dick so hard that I knew I'd have indentions from the zipper later.

"I'm greedy. I want both."

I shifted my other hand so it wrapped around her neck, my thumb lifting her chin up so I could meet her gaze.

"You are greedy. What if I want your mouth? Are you good at sucking cock, baby? Would you mind being on your knees, getting a little rug burn there as I slide my cock in and out of that pretty little mouth of yours?"

I had always talked dirty in bed. It was what I liked. I could barely remember if I had talked dirty that first night. But from the way that Rory's pupils dilated, she liked it.

And I wasn't about to stop.

"From what I can remember of your cock, I don't think it's all going to fit down my throat," she teased.

"Such a good girl. We'd find a way to make it work. A little training and you could swallow my dick. I promise you."

Her eyes darkened even more, and I leaned down to capture her lips.

"Maybe next time. Because I want to come inside that pussy of yours. You okay with that?"

She nodded. "I don't have a condom," she whispered.

"Don't worry. I do."

I had been carrying one with me ever since that kiss in the closet before. Because I was a damn asshole who couldn't keep my thoughts to myself. Even though I told myself I wasn't going to touch her again. It was all a lie. It had to be.

She pulled up my shirt again, and I took a step back, pulling it off my body with one quick motion.

"Is this what you want?

She nodded. "It's about time."

I grinned before pulling at the top of her dress. The snaps popped open, and I held the arms of the dress down so it pinned her slightly.

"Look at you, having trouble moving, and your breasts are just here for me. I can do whatever I want with them. Are you going to let me do what I want with them?" I asked.

She nodded tightly, her eyes wide.

"That's a good girl." I moved forward, rolling her nipples between my forefinger and thumb over her barely there, thin bra. "So sensitive. Can you come by someone just sucking on your nipples?"

She shook her head. "I can barely come with sex anyway."

She ducked her head as she said it, and I frowned. "You came that night. I don't remember much, but I remember that," I whispered, cupping her breasts with my hands.

She met my gaze again. "That was the only time."

I cursed under my breath. "Don't worry, baby. I'll make sure you come. More than once."

We were in a damn office where anybody could walk by and hear us, and our pizza was probably burning somewhere or getting cold if Kendall's team took care of it, and I didn't fucking care. I just needed her mouth, needed *her*.

And this time, it didn't feel like a betrayal. This time, it felt like something I wanted. Needed.

Because I'd been truthful with East. I was still grieving my wife, but I didn't mourn her every second of every day.

And I couldn't stay away from Rory.

I kissed her again before I undid the clasp of her bra, leaving her breasts bare to my sight.

I leaned forward, sucking one nipple into my mouth as I played with the other one with my hand. She moaned into me, and I paid special attention to her other breast, loving the way that her soft pink nipples darkened into red points.

"Like little cherries, I love plucking them," I whispered against her soft flesh. Her breasts were more than a handful, and I had big hands, and I couldn't wait to fuck them sometime.

Because yes, despite everything that I had said and thought before, I did not want this to be the only time.

Without saying another word, I went to my knees and pushed up her dress. She had on red cotton panties, and I groaned, loving the way that I could scent her arousal.

"So beautiful," I murmured. And I leaned forward, sliding her panties to the side to bare her pussy. She had shaved, all smooth and bare and wet. So I leaned forward and licked her once, twice, and before I could even hover over her clit more than once, she came, nearly falling off the edge of the desk as she did. I leaned forward, sucking at her clit, wanting to enhance the pleasure.

"Brooks!" she nearly shouted, and I looked up at her from between her legs.

"People can hear, baby girl. Be quiet."

She nodded, eyes wide, as I continued to suck at her pussy.

Needing her, I stood up, pulled out my condom, and shoved down my pants to my knees. It wasn't going to be pretty, but I couldn't wait any longer.

"Yes?" I asked, needing her to say it.

She nodded.

"The words, baby. I need the words."

"Yes," she whispered.

So I sheathed myself in a condom as her eyes widened again.

"I thought the piercings were just in my head," she breathed.

I looked down at them and grinned.

"No, they're all for you."

"Oh," she squeaked softly, eyes wide.

"Don't worry, I've got you."

I looked down between us and spit, loving the way that she gasped.

"I don't want to hurt you, baby. Don't worry. I'll take care of you."

And as I pressed myself against her entrance, I put one arm on her hip, the other wrapping her hair around my fist.

"Are you ready?"

"Just fuck me already," she sputtered, and I laughed as I shoved into her with one thrust.

She was so tight that my knees nearly buckled, but I stood there for a moment, letting her adjust to the size of me.

"Oh. I can feel... everything."

"I got you. Are you ready?" I asked softly.

"Just move," she groaned, rolling her hips.

"That's my girl," I whispered, both of us freezing for an instant at the words before I pushed them aside and pulled back out of her. As she whimpered, I slammed back home, and then we were moving, meeting thrust for thrust, the sounds in the room wet and full of heat.

She was so slick that it was easy to move in and out of her, her pussy tight enough to clamp around my cock.

I wasn't going to last long, even though I wanted to, but we didn't have time. So I moved my hand from her hair, slid it between us, and rubbed my thumb over her clit.

When she shot off again, her eyes meeting mine, I captured her shout with my mouth, hoping nobody heard, as I shoved deep one more time, coming to the point that I could barely see straight.

Part of me wanted to ditch the condom, to fill her, to brand her.

And I knew that primitive part of me needed to shut the fuck up and go away.

But it was all I could do just to hold her as my cock twitched inside her, and we both stood there. We both lay into one another, panting, sweaty, knowing everything had changed.

CHAPTER EIGHT
RORY

"I can't find my shoes. Did somebody take my shoes? It had to be you, Alice. Your feet can't even fit in my shoes. You're too small. You're just a baby."

Eggs on the stove, toast in the toaster, I quickly pulled the pan off the burner and moved towards the stairwell. "Cameron. Stop being mean to your sister. Your shoes are here by the door where you left them yesterday. Which are also next to your bag. Do we need to go over your homework?"

"I'm fine. I don't need your help." Cameron slammed her door, and I pinched the bridge of my nose, telling myself that perhaps things were getting smoother. In fact, it almost felt routine at this point to be called names and shouted at while trying to figure out how to raise two children I didn't know.

I went back to the stove and dished up the girls' breakfast. I didn't always make eggs and toast with fruit for breakfast, but since I hadn't been able to sleep the night before, I had woken up early with extra energy. Laundry was already in the washer, the dishwasher was unloaded, breakfast was ready, and my tablet was on the table since I had been working on the children's book illustrations before the girls had even gotten up.

It had been nearly twenty-four hours since I had had sex with Brooks.

Sex on a desk where he had talked so dirty I had nearly come just from his words alone.

And then he had disposed of the condom, taking the trash out completely after kissing me softly on the mouth and leaving me to get fixed up. I had needed to center myself, and we had parted ways, forgetting our pizzas completely.

And we hadn't talked about it. Because why would the two of us talk about it.

I knew that talk would come soon. I had fretted over it all night, hence why I hadn't slept at all. It was fine; I was just going to have to deal with it later. Because the girls came first. That was going to be the refrain for the rest of my life.

I set the fruit on the kitchen island, staggering.

For the rest of my life.

These girls were going to need me for the rest of my life. This wasn't just a few months to get used to this new feeling. This would be college applications and moms and boyfriends. Weddings and moving out and college. This was beyond hurt knees and trying to make sure that they liked the color of their new comforter. This was a life. Three lives.

And I missed my sister beyond reason. Well, I had missed my sister long before everything had changed.

And I never got to say goodbye.

Realizing a tear had slid down my cheek, I cleared my throat. "Girls. Breakfast. Please come downstairs and eat. And then we can go over everything that we need to for the morning."

The sound of socked feet on stairs echoed through the kitchen as Alice came down then, a smile on her face.

However, from the red-rimmed eyes and swollen cheeks, I knew that smile wasn't truly there.

"Alice? What's wrong?"

She didn't say anything. Instead, her smile fell, and she climbed up onto the bar stool. "Nothing. Thank you for making breakfast, Aunt Rory."

Her voice was so soft that I had to swallow hard so I didn't cry right along with her.

"If you're sure. I'm here if you want to talk."

"I'm okay," she whispered.

I ran my hand over her hair and caught my fingers in a tangle. With a sigh, I picked up the brush on the other table behind me and worked out the tangle as Alice ate.

"Do you want a braid, a ponytail, or do you want it down?"

"Can you do one of those crown braid things?" she asked, her eyes wide as she looked over at me.

I nodded. "Yes, but it might not be perfect. I'm still learning. Is that okay?"

"I don't mind. Mom used to do them."

I pushed another lump down my throat as I picked up the strands of her hair and began the braid.

"I remember. She would braid my hair too. She was always better at braiding my hair than I was at hers."

"You look so much like Mom. And when you woke me up this morning, I thought it was Mommy coming back to tell me that everything was okay. But it's not okay. Mommy and Daddy aren't coming back. And I try to be a big girl. Because Cameron said only babies cry. But I miss them so much. And I thought just for that moment that they were okay. And that we were just visiting you. And then I felt sad because I don't want to leave you either."

Tears were freely flowing down her cheeks then, and I finished the braid before holding her to my chest.

"Oh, Alice. I miss your mom so much. I'm sorry. I'm sorry I can't fix everything. But I'm here. I know I'm not the same, and I don't want to be the same. But I love you, okay? Do you know that? I've always loved you."

"I know. Mommy used to whisper it... when Daddy wasn't around."

My heart squeezed as if in a vise, and I let out a shaky breath before pulling back to finish Alice's hair.

"I loved your mom."

"Because she was your sister, like Cameron is my sister. But I bet you guys were nicer," she pouted, tears long gone.

"We fought. A lot. But we were also the same age so we had the same classes, and our mom kept dressing us the same."

"I'm not ever going to be the same as Cameron."

"And that's okay. You can be Alice. I like Alice."

I looked over at the now cooling eggs on the full plate beside Alice's and called out to Cameron again.

The not-yet-a-teenager sigh echoed once more, and Cameron stomped her way down the stairs.

"I don't even like eggs," she growled as she forced herself into the chair and bit into a piece of toast.

She had loved eggs the day before, so I didn't know

what I was supposed to say then. Looking at Alice, Cameron glared at me.

"Why did you make Alice cry?"

"She didn't. It was about Mommy."

"Don't talk about Mom."

"Alice is allowed to talk about your parents as much as she wants to. So are you. It's good for us to."

"You're not my therapist."

"No, I'm your aunt. Your guardian. And at some point, you're going to have to understand that. That I'm the adult, and you have to stop talking to me like this, Cameron."

"I'm not talking to you anyway."

"Stop being a meanie," Alice added in.

I patted Alice's shoulder. "Don't be mean to your sister either. It's okay. We're going to find a balance."

"I don't want to find a balance. I just want to go home."

"I know you do, baby. But this is our home now. And I don't know how to make it better other than telling you I'm here. Okay?"

"I'm not your baby," Cameron snapped, but she finished her eggs and fruit.

I looked at the clock and realized we were out of time. The bus did pick up at the end of the street, but I was going to drop them off today because I was worried about the two of them. I felt like I wasn't spending enough time with them or perhaps spending too much time.

They had only spent the night at Alexis' twice, and I wasn't sure how the other woman had handled all of those children. But Alice had had a fun time, and Cameron apparently hadn't acted out.

No, she only saved that for me.

Thankfully, she seemed to be respectful to her teachers, but I wasn't sure if they were making friends or not.

I was trying to figure it out, trying to figure all of this out. But this wasn't the life I had signed up for. Everything was falling through my fingers, and I couldn't keep up.

But I did not have time to wallow. Instead, I put their dishes into the sink as the girls went to brush their teeth one more time, and we headed out.

Since there were boxes in the garage, things I wasn't sure what to do with, I had parked in the driveway the night before. The girls moved ahead of me as I locked the door behind me, and I froze as Alice ran off to the side.

"Mr. Brooks! Did you see my hair? Aunt Rory did it for me. It's a braid, just like Mommy did. Do you like it?"

I forced myself to move forward, past the front porch, so I could watch the scene in front of me.

Cameron stood by the car, arms folded in front of her, but there was a blush on her cheeks as she looked up at Brooks. Well, that was going to be something I'd have to deal with later. However, Alice had her new best friend wrapped around her finger.

To the point that Brooks picked her up with one easy movement, saddled her on his hip, and walked towards us.

"The braid looks pretty, Ms. Alice. Your aunt did a good job." Brooks met my gaze then, and my throat tightened. Memories of exactly what we had done the night before slammed into me, and I told myself that I needed to stop thinking.

I didn't know what was going to happen next, but wallowing at this moment wasn't going to help anything, and frankly, the girls saw too much.

Because they'd already wondered why I had been so out of it after I picked them up after the pizza party.

I knew that my friends were trying to give me any help that they could by taking the girls for some moments, ensuring that I had some time to myself, and yet, it seemed like I wasn't making good decisions when I had that time alone.

"Come on, girls, we have to get to school now. I have two schools to drop you off at."

"No bus today?" Brooks asked as he set Alice down.

"Buses are for losers," Cameron said with her chin held high.

I leaned forward. "Or buses are for kids that are lucky enough to be in a place with one. Or maybe their parents are working."

"Whatever." Cameron got into the SUV as Alice waved back to Brooks and settled into the back next to her.

That left me alone with Brooks in my front yard, throat tight, wondering what the hell I was supposed to say.

"At least she seems to be talking to you with the same attitude she talks to me."

Brooks's lips twitched. "Good to know I'm one of the lucky few. Have a good day, Rory."

I blinked as he turned away from me, heading to his truck, and I had to wonder why I should be disappointed. It wasn't like we were in a relationship. Not really. Or not at all. Why was I disappointed that he hadn't touched me or leaned forward to brush his lips along mine? He wouldn't have done it in front of the girls anyway.

I needed to get my head out of the clouds and back to the reality that was my new life.

I pushed thoughts of Brooks away and popped into the SUV, forcing myself to pay attention to the road. I dropped the girls off, Alice happier than she had been that morning, Cameron still quiet. But each of the girls had walked off to a group of kids that seemed trustworthy. I didn't know, but perhaps I should try to wheedle out the other kids' names a little bit harder than I had been trying to. Was I supposed to talk to their parents? Were there supposed to be play dates? What did parents do?

With a sigh, I made my way back to my house and pulled into the driveway. Brooks's truck was gone, and I let out a breath.

Well, at least I didn't have to deal with that.

I made my way back inside and got to work. I had a deadline coming up and income to make.

My finances were fine, at least for now. But I needed to start the girls' college funds over again since they had lost them in the will. And that meant everything just took longer than it should.

Thankfully the Wilders knew people and were brilliant themselves, and were helping me figure things out. But at some point, I needed to stop leaning on them for everything.

We were a party of three now, and even if that broke my heart and shattered me into a million pieces, I was just going to have to deal with it.

I got a good three hours of work in when the doorbell rang. I nearly knocked over my now cold coffee at the sound but made my way to the door.

Ava walked in, brows raised, and I froze.

"Hi."

"You had sex."

I blinked, my mind going in a thousand different directions. I wasn't sure how this was possible.

"Did you hear?"

"I know your face after you have sex. And I was just here to see if you were okay after leaving the pizza thing early last night. However, what do you mean, did I hear? Oh my God. Did you have sex at Singles' Night?"

"Well. Maybe. Um."

"You know what, I think it's time for a mimosa. Or wine. Or something."

"Ava. I'm working."

"Well, if you're not going to tell me what happened, I'll have to liquor you up to get it out of you."

"I had sex with Brooks," I blurted, and Ava stood there, blinking.

"So it wasn't with Callum."

"Of course not."

"Well, I was worried."

"Why would you be worried?" I asked.

"Because I like Callum, but not for you. You guys just seem like you would be friends. And from what Briar tells me, Callum has a whole set of issues up in Ashford Creek. And I know you have enough drama now. But Brooks? Oh my God. Finally."

"What do you mean finally?"

"You guys have been giving each other loony eyes since I first got here. I remember that meeting where you two already knew each other. And I have been tight-lipped this entire time, waiting for you to tell me. But first, you had sex with Brooks. Was it good? No, don't tell me. Of course, it was good. He's a Wilder. Oh my God. It's my brother-in-law."

I blinked at her before I burst out laughing.

"Thank you for alleviating some of the stress of what just happened."

"What do you mean some? Tell me everything."

"There's not much to tell," I lied. "We went to the pizza thing, then we walked down the hall and had sex in the office. Everything's fine."

"You had sex in the office? Which office? I need to know it all."

And so I told her, not quite in detail, but when I mentioned the piercing, Ava's mouth dropped open, and she squealed. "I knew it. I knew Brooks was the kinky one."

"How on earth did you know that?"

"The quiet ones always are."

"If that's what you think. I don't think it was that kinky."

"He's a dirty talker? It's kinky. But Wyatt can be the same."

"I don't know if I want to know about your sex life with your husband."

"Well, I want to know a little bit about your sex life. So Brooks. What does this mean?"

"I have no idea."

"So you guys had sex for the first time and didn't talk about it. That sounds about right for the Wilders. What are you going to say when you see him next?"

I looked down at my hands and realized that I was squeezing them together so tight my knuckles had turned white. I forced myself to relax them and let out a breath. "That wasn't exactly the first time we had had sex."

Ava screamed and rushed forward to shake me by the shoulders.

"You had sex before this? When. I thought you guys had only kissed. Quit holding out on me."

"It wasn't here. It was before."

"So you guys *knew* knew each other. Wait. How long before?"

"About four years ago. Do you remember when Beth finally cut me off, and I realized I wasn't going to see the girls or her again? And Mom and Dad were gone, and I was flying out again to deal with things?"

"I remember. And I was dealing with my now ex-husband and all his bullshit at the time, so I couldn't go with you. Plus, Faith was sick at the time. Just a baby."

"It was that night. We got drunk at the airport bar, barely exchanged names, and I thought I would never see him again. And then it turns out he's your brother-in-law, and I don't know what I'm supposed to do. Because I keep telling myself that I shouldn't be with him, I shouldn't want him, but I can't stop."

Ava's face paled, and I cleared my throat. "So you agree?"

"No. I mean, I don't think that you guys are wrong for each other. But I remember that day. The exact date, Rory."

I stiffened, leaning against the back of the couch since we both stood in the living room. "Why do you remember that date, Ava?"

"Because that was the first anniversary of Brooks losing his wife, Rory."

I took a step back, my hand on my chest as it beat

rapidly. "Oh my God. No wonder he hates me." Tears pricked at my eyes, and I remembered him that night. The haggard look, the broken betrayal on his face.

The first anniversary of losing his wife and he had drunken sex with a random woman who turned out not to be so random.

"He doesn't hate you, Rory," Ava whispered.

"I don't hate you," a deep voice growled behind me, and I whirled, nearly falling over my feet.

"What are you doing here?" I gasped.

"The door was unlocked," he answered simply.

"That's not an answer."

"You know what, I'm just going to go," Ava said as she scampered away, out of reach of my hand as I tried to grab for her. The door slammed behind her, and I stood there in front of Brooks, wondering what the hell I was supposed to say.

"I don't hate you, Rory. I hated myself for a while, but not because of you."

The tears finally fell, and I angrily wiped them away. "Why didn't you tell me? About it being the anniversary? No wonder you looked at me later when you saw me like I was a memory you wanted to forget."

"But it wasn't you," Brooks snarled as he moved forward. He wiped his thumb along my cheek and then looked down at the wetness. "It wasn't you."

"Then what was it?" I asked softly.

"That night, I needed to drink my way out of memories. I thought I had been handling the loss well. Amara had been sick for a while. We knew it was coming. It wasn't a surprise. And yet, it felt like a gut punch. As if part of me had hoped that the cancer hadn't spread. But it had, and she was gone. And I'd been dealing with it in an analytical way because that was how I dealt with things. And then I didn't deal. And then I saw you."

Amara. Her name had been Amara. I had known that, at least on the periphery. I had known she had died of cancer that had spread far too quickly. But never because Brooks had told me. I didn't know if I was supposed to lean forward and hold him or move away so he could have space. Once again it felt like this wasn't my life, and I was failing in every level.

"When I saw you again here, it reminded me of that night. Because part of me thought that I had cheated on my wife." I opened my mouth to say something, but he put his fingers over my lips. "I was wrong. I was dealing with grief, and I wasn't doing it well. And I was wrong. It's not cheating on my wife. I know that now. But it took me a while to get there. So what we did last night wasn't cheating." His hands fell from my lips, and I swallowed hard.

"Then what was it?"

"I have no fucking clue," he said, his lips twitching.

I smiled right along with him, though I wasn't sure either one of us truly saw the humor in this.

"Rory, I have no idea what the hell I'm doing. I am trying not to be an asshole, and yet every time I'm around you, I can't help being a colossal jerk."

"You are kind of growly when I'm around."

"It's because I want you, and part of me told myself that I wasn't allowed to want you. But I promised Amara that I would try."

I frowned. "You what?"

"My wife made me promise that, when she was gone, I wouldn't become the grouchy loner who never saw another human being. And I would try again. And I have tried my hardest to break that promise. But I can't stop thinking about you, Rory."

Mind whirling at the revelation, I tried to come up with words, but I had nothing.

To say this was complicated would be an understatement.

"I have the girls, and there's the Wilders, and now this, no matter what we do, we're going to end up hurting each other."

"Maybe not," he said. "Because ignoring this isn't working."

"It's not working, but we could still try harder," I whispered. "Because I don't want to get hurt. And I don't want to hurt you. But I feel like we're just setting each other up for that."

"No, we try not to. Okay?"

"I don't think okay is what this is, but I'll try. Because you're right, ignoring this isn't working."

And then he laid his lips on mine, and I was lost.

CHAPTER NINE
BROOKS

ME

The girls get to school okay?

RORY

Yes. And no fighting over homework today. I think it's a miracle.

ME

Better knock on wood if you're truly going to believe that.

RORY

Very much so. Hold on.

ME

Did you really just knock on wood?

RORY

Of course I did. And I know you did too.

ME

Maybe.

RORY

It's only a half day though. So the girls will be home early, and we have homework, and then figuring out what sports and classes they want to start doing after school. I have no idea how moms do this every day alone.

ME

Well, I think it's because many of them don't do it alone.

ME

I can pick them up if you need.

I froze, wondering why I had said that. It wasn't as if I knew what Rory and I were to each other, but wouldn't a friend offer help? Yes, a friend would offer help. And I was their neighbor after all. It just made sense. And it wasn't as if Rory or I were any better equipped than anyone else when it came to figuring out how to navigate not only what it was between us but the girls' lives as well.

RORY

I can't ask you to do that.

I frowned, a little annoyed.

ME

You weren't asking. I was offering. You know any of us Wilders would be there for you.

RORY

I just hate asking for help.

ME

I try to never ask for help. And then I get yelled at.

RORY

That is true.

ME

Just let me know what I can do. Don't you have a conference coming up, too?

RORY

I might have to back out of that. I don't think I have enough energy to do an entire weekend away, let alone the burden of having anyone watch them. And not just asking people to do it, but the girls themselves. I don't know if I'm ready to be away from them for that long.

I swallowed hard, my fingers hovering over the keys. I needed to get back to work, especially since we had another Wilder meeting coming up in a few hours. But I couldn't help but want to continue this conversation with Rory. Though, I hated texting. Mostly because my fingers were way too big for the keys, and with every update, I swore typing got harder. Did they make the keys smaller? Or did they just decide to change it so that way some program lied to you? I wasn't sure, but I hated it.

ME

Whatever you decide, let us know. And I'll see you later?

My stomach tightened, wondering if I was ready for this, whatever this was. But I wasn't going to hurt her. I couldn't. I'd already promised myself and her that I wouldn't be that much of an asshole, so I was going to have to figure out how to do this whole being-together thing. Even though I had no idea what the hell I was doing.

RORY

I need to get back to work, but I'll think about it. And yes, I'll see you later. Have a good day, Brooks.

My fingers hovered over the screen again, but there wasn't much to say. I needed to get back to work and not think about Rory.

Not that it was going to be easy. Hell, it hadn't been easy since I had first seen her over a year ago on this property. Why would I think that once I had her under-neath me, and would be doing so again, it would be any easier?

No, it was never going to be easy.

I shook myself out of wherever the hell my mind was going and got to work. Unlike the girls, I had a full day, then a family dinner that included every Wilder in town. Usually, it would annoy me that we would have so many family dinners one after another, but for some reason, it didn't bother me that much. Okay, I could probably guess the reason at this point, but it wasn't as if I was going to spring that on the world. Nor were we hiding it.

We hadn't exactly had that conversation, but I knew that Ava knew, and therefore Wyatt knew. Which meant the rest of my family probably knew, too. Wyatt couldn't keep a secret to save his life. And, frankly, I didn't care.

Maybe it would finally get everybody off of my back when it came to setting me up. At least, I hope the hell it did.

I talked with my crew as we got to work, and ran my hand over my chest. Wondering when things got to be this way. I didn't know what I felt for Rory because I had never been in this situation before.

I had met Amara when we were young, and we had

fallen into dating. I had loved her with every ounce of my soul and still felt as if part of me would be forever crushed.

But then again, I wasn't that man anymore. It was the truth. I may not know how to date or know what to feel when it came to anyone but Amara, but I wasn't going to compare the two.

That would be a disservice to both of them.

I looked up to the sky and closed my eyes. "I hope you know what the hell I'm doing because I don't, Amara," I whispered.

I didn't talk to her often, but it didn't feel bad if I did. Rory was dealing with her own grief, something I knew I needed to pay attention to. But maybe that meant that she would understand that everything in front of us would be forever complex.

I went back to work, knowing that the expansion on this property was only a small part of the overall work to be done. I didn't want to have to travel to Austin again, and though it wasn't a long drive comparatively, it still meant that my days were longer. And with the girls, the family, and multiple jobs, finding time with Rory wasn't easy.

But I was going to find time.

And wasn't that something different?

By the time dinner rolled around, I said goodbye to

my crew, made sure my foreman was ready to go, and headed to the other side of the property in my truck rather than a golf cart and parked in front of the main building. The sun was still bright in the sky, even at this time of day since it was summer in Texas, but I was already hungry. Part of me wanted to pull out my phone and see what Rory was up to—the other part of me knew I needed to take a moment to think about what I wanted.

What *we* needed.

And I didn't know how to be part of a *we*.

"It's about time you show up," Wyatt said as I walked to the side door, and my brother held it open for me. He gave me such a wide smile that I had a feeling he knew too much.

I couldn't help but narrow my gaze. "I'm not late. I don't know why you're acting like I am."

"You're not early enough for me to rib you. I mean, I hear you have news. Lots of news."

I shoved at his shoulder as I passed him, and Wyatt just laughed.

"Well, I guess that answers that."

"It answers nothing," I growled as I made my way down the hall to the private dining room. There was already a buffet out, and I was grateful to Kendall's team. I nodded at my siblings and cousins, noticing they each already had food and were milling around. No need to eat family style tonight when we were trying out different recipes for the restaurant. My stomach rumbled, and I pulled up a plate for myself and began to pile roast chicken, scalloped potatoes, three veggies, and two rye rolls. The others were already eating, talking amongst themselves, so I went to take a seat next to Ridge and Aurora.

"You look happy," Aurora said softly, a smile in her gaze and on her face.

I let out a breath. "Hungry? Yes."

Ridge's lips twitched, but he didn't say anything.

Ava and Wyatt took a seat across from us, Faith at their side. "Hi, Uncle Brooks! I saw Alice at school today, and she said you helped her with her bike, and I wanted to say thank you too. Because you help me, and I knew you'd help her."

My family smiled at me and didn't say a thing. Bastards.

I quickly wiped my mouth with my napkin. "I did. Alice had trouble with her rear tire, and I was outside. Easy enough fix."

"Alice really likes you. And so do I. And I like mashed potatoes." And with the happiness of a kid with potatoes, she dug into her dinner as the others turned to me.

Wyatt leaned over and spoke softly. "When did it happen? How long has it been happening? And tell me everything."

"Tell you what?" Kendall asked as she skipped over to me. "Maybe why you ran out on Singles' Night and left a pizza for others to eat. Or something else?"

"You guys are ridiculous," I growled before I stuffed one of my rolls into Wyatt's mouth.

Faith burst out laughing, and the others followed.

"Please do not get Wyatt started," Ridge said as he pinched the bridge of his nose. "He's going to start singing about kissing in a tree."

"Who is kissing?" Faith asked.

"Mommy and Daddy," Ava answered.

"Blech," Faith said with a sigh. "But kissing means maybe I get a baby brother, so that's okay."

Both Wyatt and I choked on our drinks, and I quickly cleaned up the mess as my siblings laughed and Ava took Faith away to help her get a drink and "answer questions".

When the two left, Kendall followed to go sit at the nearby table with Evan and the kids. People laughed good-naturedly, and everything warmed to the point that it felt like home. I ate as others came over to the table, talked about their days, then moved around, enjoying the time together without making it feel stuffy. I leaned back after a moment, watching the way our family had changed over the past years.

I'd had this before. Not exactly this, but happiness. I'd had something that made sense. A family. Or at least the start of one. Then she was gone, and I'd told myself that I only needed this. My brothers. Cousins. Their families.

But now...

No. It was way too fucking fast.

But I wasn't ignoring her anymore.

Or us.

"Now, back to what we were talking about. From what I heard, there was kissing somewhere, and probably more," Wyatt said with a full mouth of food.

"Wyatt Wilder, what did I say about speaking with your mouth full," a familiar voice said from behind us, and we all whirled to see our parents walking through the door with a woman I didn't recognize behind them. I set my fork down and stood up, surprised to see them there but not unhappy.

I loved my parents. They'd helped me figure out the paperwork of death with Amara and had helped me figure out how to get up the next morning. Grief wasn't new to our family, not with my aunt and uncle passing away or the near misses we'd each had over time. We'd only grown closer over the years, and I knew they were thinking of officially moving away from our childhood home and staying local permanently to be near their grandkids.

But they usually warned us before they showed.

"Mom, I didn't know you were coming," Wyatt said as he set his plate on the table and ran to the couple. He picked Mom up around her waist and spun her around.

"Please do not break your mother," Dad said dryly, as I just shook my head and moved with the others to welcome them.

Taking my turn, I hugged him tightly, oddly relieved to see them. "Nice surprise. Though you both don't usually like surprises," I drawled.

"We called Eli earlier to see if there was room for us here so we could surprise you. And now we're here."

I raised a brow at my eldest cousin, who just grinned at me. He and his wife were speaking to the stranger my parents had brought, but I moved to my mother and held her closely, letting out a deep breath as I rested my chin on the top of her head. She was a tiny woman, one who I couldn't believe had raised four rambunctious, and what had to be very annoying, kids. But she fit right underneath my chin and nuzzled into me.

"I've missed you, baby boy." She pulled back, and I noticed a glint in her eyes.

"What did you do?"

"I didn't do anything. However, let me introduce you to Lauren. She works with our realtor, and well, she is a fan of Wilder Wines, so we thought we'd bring her so she didn't have to drive alone to her meeting."

Alarm bells shot off in my head, and I narrowed my gaze at my mother before putting a polite smile on for Lauren.

"Nice to meet you," I said softly, wondering what the blonde woman in front of me had been told.

Lauren gave me a strained smile. "Hi. It's nice to meet you too." She looked around the room, her eyes slightly wide. "There are so many of you."

My mother grinned. "And not all of my brood are here. Well, let me introduce you to the rest, and we'll come back to Brooks. That way you can get the full circle."

My mother gave me a look before she pulled Lauren away, and I just glared at my father.

"Really?" I asked, looking at the man who was practically my mirror image. It was nice to know what I would look like one day in a couple of decades. He had a full set of hair, gray at the temples, and was just as muscular as ever. I loved my dad. However, he was just as scheming as my mother when it came to the lives of their children. And their children included my cousins.

Because when my aunt and uncle had died, though the cousins had taken care of themselves, my parents had been there to help wherever they could.

"She's just a nice woman."

"Are you kidding me?" I growled but did my best not to be loud. I went back to my seat, my father following me.

"We just want you to be happy. And frankly, Lauren was on her way here for a meeting. And your mother waylaid her."

"And Eli mentioned this was more of a quick meal rather than a business meeting, so we didn't think it was going to be too big of a problem."

"Dad," I whispered. I didn't know how I was supposed to say that I was taken because I wasn't even sure what my and Rory's label was. But there had to be a label for me not wanting to be set up with another woman by my parents.

Lauren seemed to fit right in, though, with the others as she smiled and talked about Wilder Wines and an upcoming corporate sale.

When my mother came to the table, I ignored the questioning glance on Wyatt's face and glared at the woman who raised me.

"What? It isn't like I set you up on a date. I was just bringing a friend."

I let out a breath. "Mom, I'm... this isn't a good time." In fact, it would never be a good time when someone tried to set me up.

She leaned over and patted my hand. "It will never feel like the right time. And I'm not pushing Lauren on you. I'm just bringing a friend." She paused, her voice going soft. "I loved Amara."

"It's not that." I pinched the bridge of my nose. We were on the far end of the room where we could keep private with our voices low, and thankfully, the rest of the family was loud and boisterous as they finished dinner. As if adding random members to dinner for casual setups was par for the course. "Did I ever tell you that Amara made me promise to date again? To not fall into a pit of despair and actually love someone again? Did I tell you that?" I asked quietly.

My mom's eyes widened as they filled with tears. "No. Oh, baby..."

"I don't know what I'm doing, Mom." I blurted out the words, knowing they weren't the exact words I needed to say. I needed to talk about Rory. To tell somebody. And yet everything felt so twisted inside.

"You don't need to know what you're doing right now. And I know you're following a path that's hard. I'm sorry I'm making it harder. Everything just happened all at once, and then I was inviting her, and I couldn't warn you, and I don't know what I'm doing either."

"Mom. This really wasn't a good time, though," I said after a moment.

"What wasn't a good time?" Lauren said as she came up to me, looking statuesque in her perfectly cut suit and bright smile. She really was a beautiful woman, but she did nothing for me.

No, Rory was the only one that did that to me these days.

And I wasn't sure what to do with that.

My mother beamed up at Lauren, but I saw the tension in her shoulders now. "I'm annoying my son like usual. Here, Lauren, take my seat, and I'll get something to eat. Brooks, entertain her while I do that then hug my grandbabies."

She was so smooth about it that I couldn't protest without being a jerk, and then, somehow, Lauren was sitting next to me at the table, and Wyatt and Ava glared at me over the others' heads. From how people were reacting, it seemed that not everyone knew about me and Rory. Not yet.

And I had a feeling I was going to hear an earful if I didn't fix this. Soon.

Lauren blinked at me, shaking her head. "I love your mother, Brooks. But wow. I have no idea how I found myself in their car with them, let alone at a family dinner with you. I'm sorry. I'm totally not here to hit on you or anything. Promise. I really just wanted to see the place that made my favorite wine since I needed to come out to San Antonio anyway."

I let out a breath at her wince, feeling awkward as hell. "I'm going to be blunt with you. Usually, I'd beat around the bush, but frankly, I've had a long day. It's not your fault that my mother and the rest of my family keeps trying to set me up with women." I cleared my throat. "I lost my wife four years ago now, and they are all doing their best to help me move on. Too bad they don't get that I am fine figuring things out on my own."

Lauren's eyes widened, and she leaned forward, setting her hand on my forearm. "I am so sorry about your wife. And... well, I don't have any words. I'll try to let your mother know both of our feelings about that. It's nice to meet you, Brooks Wilder. And I'm truly sorry for your loss."

I opened my mouth to mention I wasn't free, but then the hairs on the back of my neck stood on end. I paused as I looked to see who stood in the doorway. Rory stood there, a hand on Alice's shoulder, Cameron on her other side.

My gut clenched at the look on Rory's face when she noticed where Lauren's hand was.

"Oh. Well." Rory cleared her throat. "The girls and I were just popping up to say hello on our way home. Sorry for the surprise."

My parents looked between us as my mom's eyes widened, and my dad cursed under his breath. Each of my other family members might have had their own reactions, but I couldn't pay attention to them. Instead, I stood up and walked right to her, throat tight.

"Hey, girls. I didn't know you'd be at the Inn today. Did you enjoy dinner?" I asked.

"It was fine," Cameron said softly as Alice just smiled up at me.

"Come join us for dessert," I offered. "Okay?" I looked into Rory's gaze, but she merely blinked at me.

Then she looked toward Lauren, who had also stood, her face pale.

"Thank you for the offer, but we have to head back home. School night. Say goodnight to the Wilders, girls."

I couldn't hear what anyone was saying, not with the roaring in my ears, but as I reached out for her, she took a step back. Then, in a blink, the three were gone, and I couldn't move. The idiot I was.

I cursed under my breath. "No. I need to fix this."

"Yes, you fucking do," Wyatt growled.

"What's going on?" Faith asked, but the others pulled the kids into other conversations about desserts.

My mom moved to my side, hands clenched in front of her. "Oh damn. I am so sorry, Brooks. I didn't know."

"You didn't, nobody knew." I cleared my throat and looked at my family members, who happened to still be in the room. "I've got to go. But seriously? I'm seeing Rory. Please stop setting me up on dates. Please stop making it weird. Because it's already hard enough," I growled, realizing that I didn't usually share my thoughts or feelings, and I didn't really feel like doing it right now. But I'd seen the hurt on Rory's face, and I had to wonder what exactly she had seen before I had noticed her.

Lauren waved slightly and I knew she had to be feeling so far out of the loop it wasn't even funny. "If it helps, I truly came here because I love your parents and Wilder Wines, so I'm not going to make it weird. If you need me to talk to her to let her know that I've literally spoken six sentences to you, I will."

I snorted, wondering why the hell this was my life before I turned and ran. The others all spoke at once, but I ignored them, knowing I needed to find Rory. I didn't know what I felt for Rory other than I had made a promise. And I wasn't about to fuck this up. And that meant I needed to make sure that I hadn't just pushed away the one woman who could stand me after all these years.

CHAPTER TEN
RORY

There was an odd echoing sound between my ears, but I ignored it. Perhaps it wasn't an echo, a buzzing? I wasn't sure, but I was going to pretend it didn't exist while I quickly went through the evening's chores and checklists.

The drive back to the house from the Wilder property had been awkward, mostly because even Alice had noticed the tension.

I had done all in my power to pretend that I wasn't breaking inside, wondering how stupid I could possibly be. It wasn't as if we had said we were exclusive. Or had we? I had thought maybe we had. He had been territorial and demanding, but maybe that was just how Brooks was. And I had read too much into it. Just like I always did. And frankly, I didn't have time to even worry about men. I had two girls who needed me, a job that was overwhelming because I was slightly behind, and a future that was so grayed out that I wasn't even sure how I was supposed to function.

So, in the end, I didn't need to worry about anyone else, but wondering what the heck I was going to do.

At least when it came to my family.

Because the girls and I were family. We were the only ones left, and though that was a kick in the gut, I was just going to focus on what I could handle. Even though I wasn't sure I could even handle this.

"Can we have ice cream?" Alice asked as she bounced on her toes.

I shook my head. "You had ice cream at the restaurant. Remember?" I reminded, trying to keep my voice light. Alice, though, kept staring at my face, and I knew she was searching for something. Maybe answers? Well, it wasn't as if I could give them to her. I barely had them for myself.

"It was really good ice cream."

My lips twitched. "Better than what we have. They make it fresh."

"Why didn't we stay? I thought that they were your friends," Cameron asked, frowning at me.

I played with the hem of my sleeve and shrugged.

"It was a family thing, and we have things to do. Plus, you guys have school tomorrow. In other words, we should get ready for bed. Go brush your teeth and your hair, and I will be upstairs to help tuck you guys in soon."

"I don't need to be tucked in. And it didn't look like all family. I didn't recognize that one woman."

I met Cameron's gaze and tilted my head, studying her. "We had to come home anyway. It's fine," I lied.

Because that woman wasn't family. And she had her hands on Brooks. Perhaps I was the idiot, or perhaps it was something I would have to deal with later. But not with a child who wasn't even a teenager yet.

"Is Brooks going to come by tomorrow? I really like him. He promised that he would help me figure out if I want to do soccer or football," Alice said with a grin.

"Girls don't do football," Cameron snapped.

At the sound of Brooks's name, I ran my hand over my heart.

"First, girls can totally play football. Especially in this area. There's a whole team for it, and if that's what Alice wants to do, or if that's something you want to do, Cameron, you can. Second, I don't know if Brooks is coming over, but we can go over everything that you'd like to do. Both of you. We have another week until we have to finalize signing up for teams because we're new in town. I will make sure that you guys can do everything that we possibly can, but please know that I'm just one person, and I'm going to try to get you everywhere."

"I'm just really excited to play and make new friends," Alice said as she wrapped her arms around me.

Cameron didn't say anything.

The doorbell rang, and Cameron met my gaze, an odd sense of fear in her eyes.

I didn't understand it for a moment, until it clicked.

Because the last time someone had rang her doorbell near the end of the night, people showed up to tell her that her parents were gone.

Cameron's eyes went impossibly large, grief tinging edges, and I reached out, wanting to comfort her. She immediately took a step back, the connection between us broken, as Alice ran towards the door.

"I'll get it!"

Alarmed, considering the sun had set and it could have been anyone at the door, I ran behind her.

"No, wait! You know the rules. You make sure I answer the door first."

But Alice was already there, swinging the door open.

"Brooks! You're here. Aunt Rory wasn't sure when you were going to be here. But now that you're here. I'm so glad." She wrapped her arms around his legs, and he leaned down to pick her up and plop her on his hip like he had done so many times prior.

"Well, hi there. That's a welcome." He rubbed his cheek on the top of Alice's head, and she laughed, even though Alice was far too big to be carried like that. I didn't think either one of them cared.

Brooks met my gaze, and I swallowed hard, wanting to reach out and touch him, wanting to reach out and push him away.

That was the problem, wasn't it? I never knew what to do when it came to Brooks Wilder. And seeing him with that other woman had broken something inside me. I had already told myself that this was too much. That I wouldn't continue to make poor decisions. And now here I was, in such a vulnerable position that there was no coming back from it.

"So, can you come over tomorrow so we can talk about sports? I also want to learn how to draw like Aunt Rory, but Aunt Rory said that girls are allowed to play football. Is that really true?"

He blinked at me as if pulling himself out of his thoughts like I was trying to do and then looked down at Alice. "That's right. You can play football if you want."

For some reason, that inevitably made me think of the last time I had seen Brooks play football. Shirtless, sweaty, and I was losing my damn mind all over again.

I swallowed hard, pushing all thoughts of him out of my mind, even though it literally couldn't happen since he was in front of me.

This man was a menace to my self-control.

"What are you doing here?" Cameron asked as the young girl stood by my side and folded her arms over her chest.

Apparently, Cameron was going to defend me over whatever she thought had happened, and part of me wanted to warm up at that moment. Maybe it was the first time we were on the same side. However, there shouldn't be sides at this moment. Because I didn't want the girls to get in the middle of this. And this is why I shouldn't have gotten involved with Brooks. Everything was such a mess.

But he had let that other woman touch him. It looked as if they were on a date or at least comfortable enough to be around his family.

And I hadn't been there. Had I even been invited? I wasn't sure. I was too focused on so many other things, but I couldn't help but let that image of that beautiful woman and Brooks sitting so close to one another ingrain itself onto my memory. I just wanted him to leave. So it would be easier to forget him. And maybe easier to breathe.

"Cameron, watch your tone, please," I said after a moment, realizing that Cameron had been just as rude as I wanted to be at that moment.

Brooks raised a brow but cleared his throat as he set Alice down. "I'm here to talk to your aunt. I think we have a few things to say to one another."

"It's late, and I need to get the girls ready for bed."

"Then I'll wait in the living room."

"Oh, you should read a story with us. Please?" Alice asked as she tugged him in.

Alice was seven now and still liked being read to. I didn't know if my sister had done this for her. They had mentioned casually that she had used to. But I didn't know what my sister and brother-in-law had done for the girls in the years we had been apart from each other. I didn't know what had changed, other than we were finding our own rhythm. One where sometimes we cried, sometimes we broke down, sometimes we failed, but we were figuring it out.

Only I wasn't sure I was doing it well enough at this moment.

"Oh, Brooks, you don't—"

"I'd be honored to," Brooks interrupted as he looked down at Alice and then at me. "Cameron, do you get a story, too?"

"I'm twelve. I can read on my own."

"I can read, too, but it's fun to hear Aunt Rory do the voices. Do you do the voices?" Alice asked Brooks.

Brooks shrugged. "Not really. But I can practice."

"Fine, but I want to hear too," Cameron muttered as she turned on her heels and went upstairs, presumably to get in her pajamas.

My lips twitched because Cameron did indeed have a little crush on Brooks, in the way that twelve-year-olds did, and maybe a story would calm her down.

But it wasn't going to do anything to help me in this situation.

"Alice, why don't you get in your pajamas and brush your teeth, and we'll meet you with whatever book you choose."

"Okay. Are you sure you're not leaving early? Are you sure you're going to stay?" Alice asked, her gaze intent on Brooks.

He nodded tightly, and I saw the pain on both of

their faces. None of us were strangers to loss or broken promises, but we were trying.

At least, I felt we had been.

Alice ran upstairs after her sister, leaving me alone in the entryway with Brooks. The man I was falling for, and I had no idea why.

"It wasn't what you thought," Brooks whispered.

I snorted before taking off my reading glasses, having not realized I had left them on. "Really? That's what you're going with?"

"Lauren was just there—"

"So her name is Lauren. I hope you two will be very happy. Because I'm not playing the jealous harpy or whatever this was supposed to be. I'm sorry for thinking this was something more than it was."

Brooks was right in front of me then, hand on the back of my neck, the other lifting up to rub his thumb over my bottom lip.

"Don't touch me," I whispered, my body shivering. For more? Or for him to leave. The problem was I didn't know.

"Listen. My parents brought her here to introduce her to me because they didn't know."

"Know what?" I asked, my heart pounding in my chest. That slight twinge of hope at his words threatened, and I refused to let it take root. I refused to want any more than I had.

"I told everyone in that room that I was taken. That you and I were seeing each other. I realized I don't know what the hell we're doing, and I'm not good at this, but I wasn't about to let you be hurt by something as stupid as a woman saying she was sorry about my loss."

I tried to take a step back, but his hold tightened. "I don't want her. I want you."

"She touched you," I whispered. "And I don't like being territorial."

"Callum looks at you, and I want to rip his face off. Do you want to talk about territorial?" he asked, his voice low with a growl that went straight to my core. I pressed my thighs together, and his eyes darkened.

"It's fine. I guess I was wrong."

"It's not fine," he bit out. "I'm sorry. I keep hurting you, and I don't mean to."

And just like that, I melted. For him, for what could have been. Because I was a fool.

"I'm sorry, too. For running. I'm just a little tender it seems."

"We'll fix that. And I'll show you how sorry I am soon."

I swallowed hard and took a step back at the sound

of Alice's footsteps at the top of the stairs. "I guess we should go read to them."

"I guess so. What do seven-year-old girls read these days?"

"I think it varies, but Cameron's going to be involved too."

"Why do I feel like I should be worried?"

"You really should be. Come on." I held out my hand, and he took it, and all felt right. Or maybe, all felt as if I hadn't taken a step that I wasn't ready for.

We walked up to Alice's room, and I quickly let go of his hand. I didn't know what the girls knew, and frankly, I wasn't good at dating, let alone dating as a guardian. When were you supposed to sit the girls down and explain what you were doing with another man? Let alone, when you didn't know what you were doing. Being a parent was damn hard, and I hadn't read a rule book about this. There had to be an outline or something, a how-to. Of course, there were probably a million books on it, but nothing about this situation.

"How about this one? We don't need to read the whole thing."

"You can't read the whole thing in a night," Cameron said with a roll of her eyes. She sat at the end of Alice's bed, back to the wall. Alice sat with her back to the headboard, book in hand. They both smelled of mint, with fresh faces, and looked so sweet and innocent.

The same little girls who had cried the night before when each had had a nightmare and hadn't wanted to tell the other. But each had held one another while I had held them.

We were navigating this space, and maybe I wasn't failing completely.

Brooks pushed past me and took a seat at the edge of Alice's bed. I scrambled into the small space at the edge next to Cameron and was grateful when she didn't pull away. Instead, she snuggled into me as Alice lifted Brooks's arm to sink into his side, and I wanted to take a photo, to snap a picture of this moment forever.

I listened with half an ear as Brooks's deep grumble of a voice soothed Alice to sleep in his side, her bow-mouth parted as she slightly snored. Cameron dozed lightly, and as thirty minutes passed, and we went further than a chapter, Brooks set the book down on the nightstand, and I gently tugged Cameron off the bed as Brooks tucked Alice in, turning off the nightlight. I stood at the doorway, Cameron leaning into me, as we watched Brooks lean down to brush a kiss over the top of Alice's head before he turned towards us.

I mouthed that I would be right back and walked Cameron to her room.

She yawned quietly and looked at me with an odd look on her face.

"What is it?" I asked, keeping my voice low.

"Are you and Brooks together?" she asked.

I swallowed hard and promised myself that I would never lie to her. "Yes, but it's still new."

She frowned and nodded. "I like him."

And with that, she tucked herself in, and I knew better than to help her. It would just start a fight, especially when she had been so nice just now. But I turned off her light, grateful for this odd semblance of normalcy in a world that was anything but normal.

And then I was walking to my room, Brooks behind me. Throat tight, I closed the door behind both of us and let out a deep breath.

"That was weird," I said with a soft laugh.

"Tell me about it. Although, I did get some practice by reading to Faith."

"You're better at it than I am."

"I don't believe that. You draw stories for a living. I bet you have more imagination than you think."

I shook my head and took a step away from him, needing to breathe. It was hard to even think when he was around, Or perhaps that was just something that he did to me.

"I don't know. I think the girls liked listening to you read." I looked down at my hands. "So did I."

"I am sorry, you know. For how it looked. And for blurting out in front of everybody that we were dating. Considering we hadn't really said those words yet."

A smile stretched over my face, imagining that. "Well, at least you had to deal with the awkwardness with that. As I ran away with the girls to the car."

"You guys did scurry quite quickly."

"We did not scurry," I whispered, knowing that even though we were on the other side of the hall, we had to be quiet.

Brooks's gaze went to my lips, and my tongue darted out as if it had a mind of its own.

"I don't want to hide this. Whatever this is," he said after a moment.

"I think blurting it out to your family sort of excludes the whole hiding it thing," I said with a small half-laugh.

"True." He stepped forward, his thumb tracing along my jaw. "I haven't been very good about figuring out what to do with you, have I?"

"I wasn't aware you had to do something with me?"

"I don't date. Or at least I haven't. Not since..."

I nodded, throat tight. "I haven't dated since Anthony."

Brooks's eyes narrowed. "And who the hell is that?"

I snorted. "Someone that doesn't mean anything to me. It has been a long while since I've been in a relationship. And I didn't know how to do the whole dating thing when I didn't have two kids to take care of."

"So we'll figure this out together. But I think that means I should kiss you now."

"Oh? That's what you think?"

"Yes. And I should hold your hand when we're in public. And maybe take you out. Have I ever taken you out?"

I shook my head. "No. But it's not like we have time for that. You have how many jobs within your one job? And with the girls, and our friends, who happen to be your family, I don't think there's much time for that at all."

"Then we'll make time. Because if I'm going to figure this whole path out, I might as well do it with purpose."

"Oh. I like you with purpose."

"Good."

And then he leaned forward, his lips on mine. I groaned into him, hooking my fingers in his belt loops.

He pulled away, leaving me wanting.

"We're going to have to be quiet if we do this."

My eyes widened. "I've never actually had sex with other people in the house before."

"I promise I'll be gentle."

I snorted. "I don't think you know how to be gentle."

"I could. If I tried. If that's what you wanted."

I shook my head. "You might have to gag me," I teased.

This time, it was Brooks who'd groaned before he picked me up by my hips and carried me to the bed.

I wrapped my legs around his waist, kissing him wholeheartedly.

If I was going to make this mistake, I might as well lean into it. Brooks Wilder was going to break my heart, but for now, I could just live in the moment.

I didn't do that often enough.

He set me down at the edge of the bed, exploring my mouth with his own as if he was a man dying of hunger and I was his feast. When he tugged at my shirt, I released my hands so he could pull it over my head. He undid my bra in a move that left me gasping as my breasts fell heavy into his hands. He cupped them, pinching my nipples in between his thumb and forefinger. I gasped again, and he raised a brow at me. I put my hand over my mouth, keeping myself quiet as he lowered his head, sucking on one nipple hard enough that I knew it would leave a bruise. And then he did it to the other nipple, and I rubbed my thighs together, my clit pulsating.

But when he turned me around, I moaned.

"Hands on the bed," he ordered.

I did so, bending over for him. His jeans-clad cock pressed hard against my backside, and I wiggled against him, needing that motion.

He chuckled roughly, and then he licked slowly up my spine.

I exhaled shakily, arching my back.

"I love this tattoo here. Every time I see it, it gets me hard. Like when you are reaching up for something, and I just get a bare glimpse. It reminds me of when you're bent over like this, and my cock is slowly sliding into you from behind. Because one day, I'm going to fuck this ass of yours and watch as your back arches just like this, and this tattoo will be exactly what I focus on. And then I'll pull out and come all over that pretty back of yours. What do you think? Do you think your tattoo will look pretty covered in my cum?" he asked, his voice so growly that I squirmed harder against his cock.

He gripped my hip, keeping me steady.

"If you make me come in my jeans, I'm going to spank that ass."

I wiggled again, and the sharp sting of his hand against my ass, even through my jeans, made me gasp.

"Face on the bed. Keep that mouth of yours closed as I show you exactly what I mean."

I lowered my face, biting down on the comforter so I wouldn't shout as loudly while he pulled down my pants with my panties all in one movement.

I was naked before him as he knelt behind me, spreading my ass cheeks.

"So fucking beautiful. Look how wet you are. Just for me?"

I nodded, mouth full of comforter as I gripped the bedding tightly. And then he was licking my cunt, exploring me with his tongue. He sucked on my clit, twisting his lips ever so slightly, nearly rocking me off the bed. But he kept me steady, spreading me as he then buried his face in my ass, licking and sucking. And when he dove back into my pussy with his tongue, I nearly came but curled my toes into my carpet, keeping myself steady. He slowly probed my asshole with his fingers, using my own fluids to wetten them, but he didn't push deeper in. Aching, I pressed back, and he chuckled.

"I think you're going to need to be a little more wet for this." He spit at me, once, twice, over my asshole, and then he was probing me again, guiding one finger deep inside and then a second. He stretched me, and my toes spread, my whole body arching for him.

"One day, you'll be ready for my cock, but not yet."

He licked at my pussy again, and then I was coming, both of us groaning. Thankfully, his face was still between my legs, muffling the sound.

And before I could blink, his jeans were off, the sound of him undoing his belt nearly making me come again.

And when the feel of his piercing against my wet pussy nearly sent me over the edge again, I moaned.

"I know we said we were both clean, and you're on birth control, but are you ready for me?" he asked, his voice soft.

"Please. Just fuck me," I whispered.

"Damn straight."

And then he was inside of me, the feel of him bare within me sending me over the edge. I could feel every single barbell touching that soft and sensitive spot deep inside. He froze, his fingers digging into my hips as I came, clenching around his cock.

And then he was moving, hard, fast, fucking me into the edge of the bed.

Before I could think, he was pulling out, and I was on my back, knees up to my shoulders, as he slid into me again.

"Look down in between us, look at me fucking you. This is you, me. No one else. Do you see that? Your pussy is begging for my cock, gripping it. Do you hear that? You're so fucking wet. So turned on just by my cock."

"It's not just your cock," I whispered, and he laughed, taking my mouth.

We both moved against one another, taking each other, my fingers dug into his shirt, and I realized he was still clothed, so I slid my hands up his back, clinging to him as he fucked me, both of us meeting gazes for once. And, in that moment, his eyes darkened again, and he whispered my name against my lips before he came, filling me with his cum.

He lay above me, hovering so he didn't crush me for a moment, as I swallowed hard.

"Well, I don't think I've come that hard in a while," I whispered.

"Same. I thought I'd last a bit longer." He kissed me softly on the mouth, once, twice, before gently playing with my breasts, as if absentmindedly just needing to touch me.

Tears pricked my gaze, and I knew this man could hurt me, but again, maybe he wouldn't.

Maybe all would be okay.

"Let me get you cleaned up, baby girl. I think I left my mark on you."

"Are you talking about bruises? Or the fact that I'm pretty sure I can feel your cum sliding out between my legs."

He laughed roughly, shaking his head. "Next time, we'll lay down a towel. As it is, somebody's going to have to lay in the wet spot."

I swallowed hard, meeting his gaze. Because that meant he was sleeping over.

Maybe this was just one more step.

We quickly cleaned each other up, and I removed my comforter, knowing I would have to wash it soon. He threw a spare quilt on top after we showered, and I pulled on pajamas, piled my hair on the top of my head, and watched as he picked up my comforter, fully dressed now, and we walked towards the laundry room downstairs by the kitchen.

I started the load, knowing I would have a long night of work ahead, when Brooks frowned at his phone.

"What's wrong?" I asked, worried that he was going to leave, and I wasn't sure what to do about it. I was already sore between my legs, but I wanted him to hold me, to be able to wake up with him at my side. It was probably a fool's dream, but it was what I wanted.

"Well, this is going to be interesting," he mumbled.

"What is it?" I asked as he went to the front door.

"Brace yourself," Brooks grumbled as he opened the door.

I blinked, knowing I was going to have to yell at that man later. Because bracing myself didn't really give me a warning for who stood at my doorway.

Brooks's parents were there, small smiles on their faces, and a hope in their gaze that worried me.

Because it matched my own.

"Mom, Dad, what are you doing here?" he asked, his voice low. "The girls are sleeping upstairs."

"That's why we texted. We didn't know if they were sleeping or not. Your truck was in her driveway, not yours, so we figured you were here."

I looked at Brooks, and he cursed under his breath. "Sorry. If we had neighbors, we would be letting the whole neighborhood know."

I rolled my eyes and waved awkwardly. "Hi. I'm Rory."

"It's so nice to meet you. I know we're barging in, but I felt so bad about how dinner ended. I'm Rebecca, and this is my husband, Carlos."

"It's nice to meet you, Rory," Brooks's dad said softly.

"Anyway, we just wanted to see Brooks, apologize

for how things went, and invite you to dinner. Not tonight, of course, it's a little late. But hopefully while we're in town?"

"Oh." I looked at Brooks, who wasn't saying a damn thing. Stupid man.

"I have the kids, and with school and everything, I'm not sure," I said, my teeth worrying my lip.

Brooks wrapped his arm around my shoulder, pulling me close. "Bring the girls. We'll get dinner. Okay, Mom and Dad? Are you guys sleeping at the resort, or do you want the keys to my house? You can have the guest room."

"Oh, don't worry about that, Brooks."

"No, you have your stuff there from last time, and I don't want you driving late. Here, take my keys. Get some sleep, and I'll be over for breakfast in the morning. Okay?"

Brooks's mom smiled so wide before she leaned forward, hugged her son hard, and then kissed my cheek, surprising me. "That sounds great. I know the girls have school tomorrow, but be prepared for cinnamon rolls. I'm sorry, I can't help it. I need to bake."

"Mom," Brooks warned, and Brooks's dad laughed.

"Just let her. She's nervous."

"Oh, stop it, Carlos. Seriously though, we'll see you in the morning. Have fun." And then they practically scampered off to Brooks's house, leaving me standing there next to the man I was definitely falling in love with, wondering what the hell had just happened.

"I would say I'm sorry about that, but I'm about to get cinnamon rolls and probably morning sex. I can't really complain."

I looked at him then, knowing yes, and I had indeed fallen in love with him.

We shut the door, and I followed him upstairs, agreeing, yes, we were probably going to have morning sex.

No, *definitely*.

CHAPTER ELEVEN
BROOKS

I sank into the couch cushions, that familiar leather-like butter. It had taken Amara and me a good month to find this couch and then three more months for it to arrive, and it was like our child. I put my feet up on the coffee table, pulled out my e-reader, and decided I was just going to read for the afternoon. Amara would be home any minute, and then we would sit and maybe put this couch to good use. After all, it was time to have another baby, at least according to Amara. One that wasn't a couch.

My lips twitched, knowing that we were also looking for a dog, one that would fit our family and would probably destroy the couch.

I pat the leather, holding back a laugh. "So sorry," I said, trying not to smile as I went back to reading.

The door opened slowly, and I looked up as the love of my life walked into the room, her auburn hair framing her face and the shoulder-length haircut she had just gotten and wasn't quite sure she liked. I thought she looked beautiful no matter what she wore. Hell, she made me hard just looking at her, but saying that didn't help her like her haircut. She'd always had flowing long hair and spent much of her fun budget on different products for it. I didn't mind because when I ran my hands through it, it made her purr.

"Hey there, babe," I said, and Amara looked at my feet on the table but didn't say anything. I frowned, setting my booted feet down on the ground, wondering why she hadn't. I liked our jabs at each other, cute ones that just meant we loved each other.

"What's wrong?" I asked, setting my book down and up by her side in a flash.

"I... it's bad, Brooks."

I swallowed hard, trying to hear what she said, but it was a garbled mess. Then we were standing in a doctor's office, explaining how stage four meant it had fully metastasized and moved to other organs. There were treatments that we could try, special programs so we could pay for it. And yet, the doctor's words were just as jumbled. I blinked, and we were sitting in the hospital room, poison being injected into my wife's port as she finally took off the cold cap, annoyed with it.

"I don't need to keep my hair. I just need to get this over with."

I leaned down to kiss her, but then the dream changed, and that sense of fear that had been with me from the moment I had seen her was not able to take root.

Now, we stood in the bathroom as she sobbed into her hands, and I finished shaving off the rest of her hair. I leaned forward, tapped her shoulder, and immediately began to shave off mine.

"Brooks. No."

"We can grow it back together. Damn it."

She looked up at me then, but there was no hope there.

But that wasn't right. She had been the hopeful one. I had been the one who had looked into the abyss and tried to evade my own pain.

We blinked, and we were back on that couch, and she was making me make a promise that I didn't want to keep.

"You have to, Brooks. Love again. That's all I'm asking. Rory's such a good person, don't you think?"

I blinked, confused as hell.

"What?"

"Your heart is so big, Brooks. You take care of everyone. And now you're taking care of Rory and those girls. They need you."

I tried to pull away, but her strength had returned, and she clutched at my wrist.

"I could never hate you, but this isn't right. This isn't what you said."

"I love you, Brooks. And I know you love me. Now, remember your promise. You said you hated me and loved me all at once because I made you promise."

I swallowed hard and reached out for Amara, but then it was Rory sitting there, her bald head cold without her cap. Her lips were chapped, her eyes sunken. And I screamed.

I shot up in the bed, heart pounding, as Rory reached for me.

"What is it?"

"Sorry. Bad dream."

She frowned, but I didn't say anything. Instead, I leaned forward and kissed her forehead, running my hand over her braid that she slept in.

"I'm going to go splash water over my face," I whispered.

"Do you want to talk about it?" she asked as she sat up next to me.

I shook my head. "No, I'll be okay."

Hurt slid over her face, and I understood it. But I wasn't about to tell her that I had pictured her in Amara's place, dying in my arms. There was no need to dive deeper into that.

Instead of heading to her bathroom to wash my face, I padded down the hallway so I could go to the kitchen and get some water. I wore sleep pants and a T-shirt, considering I was sleeping at her house. We had been doing this for a couple of weeks now, and the girls hadn't minded. In fact, they hadn't said anything. I didn't know when that was going to change, but for now, we were making it work.

This relationship.

A sound hit my ears, and I paused outside of Alice's room.

"Momma!"

I cursed under my breath and slid into Alice's room as she twisted in the sheets, tears running down her cheeks even as her eyes squeezed shut.

I sat down at the edge of the bed and turned on the lamp on the nightstand table.

"It's okay. Wake up, Alice. It's just a dream. A nightmare."

Alice shot up from bed and threw her little shaking body around me, sobbing into my shoulder.

"I miss my mommy," she muttered into me, and I

let out a shuddering breath, just running my hand up and down her back.

"I know you do, baby. I'm sorry."

"Don't go. Don't go like Mommy and Daddy."

I just held her, not making any promises. I didn't know if Rory and I were going too fast, or slow as molasses, but if I walked away because I kept having dreams that I was losing Rory just like I lost Amara, I wasn't only going to hurt the woman I was trying not to fall for. I was going to hurt this little girl and the almost teenager standing in the doorway, arms folded over her chest.

"Alice had a nightmare."

"I can handle it," Cameron said as she lifted her chin.

"But you don't have to," Rory whispered.

Cameron just shook her head and slid past her back to her room.

Rory met my gaze, sighing.

I wasn't sure how to get through to Cameron. I knew that she had to be hurting, but every time she lashed out at Rory, it hurt her. Hell, it hurt both of them. But Rory continued to take it, and that's why I had a feeling Cameron kept doing it. Because Rory wasn't going to leave, no matter how many times Cameron lashed out.

Eventually, Rory and I got Alice back to bed, and instead of heading for water or anything in the kitchen so I could get away for a moment, I followed Rory back to bed, and without a word, we fell back asleep, thankfully, dreamless.

THE NEXT DAY, INSTEAD OF TAKING MY DAY OFF OR THE GIRLS spending time outside with their friends, we were all at a wedding.

There was a major wedding taking place on the property later tonight, and a few of the crew were sick, and that meant all hands on deck to finish prep.

As the wedding planner, Alexis was in twenty places at once, giving orders like a drill sergeant, and we did whatever she needed.

There were hay bales to be moved in one area and seating moved to another. Kendall and her team were in charge of catering, and I wasn't quite sure how Kendall could do eight jobs at once, but hell, I did the same.

Even Bethany, my cousin-in-law who happened to be an Academy Award-winning actress, had her hair pulled back, a ball cap on her head to hide her face slightly, and was standing up on a ladder and working on fairy lights that had come down in the winds overnight.

Rory stood by my side, both of us working on setting out chairs for the outside evening wedding. Cameron had been helping, but now she sat on the ground near us, pouting as she stared at the book in her hands. She wasn't reading anything but glaring at it.

Alice, however, had found a few friends from school and the five of them were playing soccer in the field near us. There were adults watching, and every once in a while, Rory would keep her eye on Alice, making sure that the little girl stayed in place. Hell, I was doing the same thing.

"Okay, how many chairs does this wedding need?" Rory asked, and I shook my head.

"I have no idea. However many Alexis tells me. That's really the only answer."

Rory smiled up at me, and my heart kicked. I didn't even think twice about it; I just leaned down and brushed my lips against hers.

"Well, well, well," Ridge muttered, and Aurora shushed him before wiggling her fingers at us and going back to the main building. As she was the main pastry chef for the company, I knew she had to be either working on the wedding cake or some of the desserts that had to be served. I wasn't quite sure, as I just did what I was told.

"Ugh, why do you have to keep kissing like that. It's gross."

"Brooks and I like each other and are seeing each other. That's really all that matters," Rory answered before I could.

"I just don't think you should be doing that in public." Cameron stood up and brushed the dirt off of her jeans. "I mean, the girls that kiss boys at schools are just sluts, so I guess you are too."

"Cameron!" Rory gasped, but I pushed past her and leaned down over Cameron. She shivered back, eyes wide.

"I know you're hurting. I know that nothing is right at the moment, and everything you try to do pales in comparison to the life you thought you'd had. I get that. But right now? This is the life you're living. If you want to be bitter for the rest of your life, you're more than welcome to, but if you ever talk about Rory like that or say anything like that to her face, we're going to have a problem. And frankly, you shouldn't be calling anybody a slut."

Cameron's eyes filled with tears before she pushed at my chest and ran in the opposite direction. Because I hadn't been expecting it, I took a step back and frowned.

"Fuck. I'm sorry."

"No. I should have said something. Damn it. I need to go find her."

I nodded and watched as Rory chased after Cameron, and I shook my head.

"Everything okay?" Ava asked, frowning.

"No. Cameron keeps lashing out at Rory, and she went too far this time. But I may have towered over her and growled."

"What did she say?" Ava asked.

When I explained, she narrowed her gaze. "Good on you. Rory is too lenient sometimes, but I get it. Cameron is hurting, grieving, but at some point, there's no excuse for being rude and cruel. Because that was cruel. I'm going to go after them and see if there's anything I can do."

"Should I go too?" I asked. "Apologize?"

Ava shook her head. "No. You didn't do anything wrong. I don't know how Cameron and Alice's parents disciplined them or even raised them, but from what I can tell, they ignored them a lot. Alice clings to you like she's never had a father figure in her life, and she slid right into Rory's arms as if she's always been there. Cameron?

Cameron was old enough to know something was wrong in that family. Especially from what we can tell about the whole community. You're doing a good thing. However, we will have to have a talk at some point."

My mind whirled as I tried to figure out exactly everything that she had just said. After the word father figure, I had blanked.

"What do you mean?" I asked, scowling.

"You're dating my best friend. We're going to have to have words."

"Ava, really?"

"Somebody needs to protect her. Those girls are her only family, at least by blood. But I'm her family too." She sighed. "Just like I'm yours. So, I'm happy for you both, and just be careful. Both of you. There's a lot of tentative paths and tripwires for all of you."

And with that, she followed where the girls went, and I pinched the bridge of my nose.

"Ava go off with your woman?" Wyatt asked.

"Should I hit you or something for calling her that?" I asked as I looked up at my brother.

"No. Because you're just as much of a possessive asshole as I am."

I shrugged because he wasn't wrong.

"You have dark circles under your eyes, bro. You want to talk about it?"

I nearly shook my head but sighed. "I had a dream about Amara last night, and then somehow it turned into Rory having cancer, so not really."

Wyatt's face paled, and he cursed. "I'm sorry. Fuck."

"Pretty much. There's nothing I can do about it. I don't have to do too much dream searching and therapy to figure out why I had the dream. But it still kicked me in the ass last night. And then Alice had a nightmare about her parents, and here we are, with Cameron calling people names, sobbing far away, and I'm standing here, talking about my feelings. Which you know I love doing."

"The fact that you're even talking to me at all is progress."

"I'm fine. Yes, I'm a little lost sometimes, but it's not like it was yesterday. It's been years. I'm always going to miss her. I'm always going to think about her. But I know now that I'm not stepping out on my wife by being with Rory."

"Good. Now, are you going to tell us what you feel about her?"

"Not even a little," I said softly as I stared out to the soccer field and frowned.

"Hey, do you see Alice?" I asked, slight alarm tingling down my spine.

Wyatt looked towards the field and shook his head.

"Maybe she's over the ridge? I see the other kids, though."

"Yeah, maybe she's there. Faith is at Eli's place, right?"

"Yeah, the littles wanted to have a play date, but I knew Rory wanted Alice and Cameron close."

"Let me go find Alice. I don't know, maybe she went and followed Rory and Cameron?" I asked as I picked up my pace, jogging towards the field.

"I'll go check," Wyatt said as he ran towards the building.

I looked over the field, past the ridge, past the hill, but couldn't see the little girl.

I stopped the closest kid and did my best not to scowl. "Do you know where Alice went?" I asked.

"No," the kid said, but he raised his chin.

I raised my gaze. "You're going to want to change that answer."

"I don't have to answer to you."

"Excuse me, that's my son," a clipped voice said from my side, and I turned towards a woman with a scowl on her face and her phone in her hand.

"Sorry, I'm looking for Alice. She was out here playing. I'm one of the Wilders that owns this place, and Alice is one of ours."

"Oh. The little girl with pigtails? She was right here." She frowned, searching the field with me.

This time, a cold sweat began to trickle down my back, and I looked down at the little kid. "Do you know where she went?"

"Some of the older kids were making fun of her and called her an orphan, so she ran off. I'm sorry." His little lip quivered, his eyes filling, and I wanted to shout, to do something, to find those kids and shake them, but instead, icy cold fear slammed into me.

"Jacob." The woman looked at me. "I'm so sorry. I'll help you look. And I'll have a talk with him."

"I don't care," I said as I kept moving, searching for Alice.

I pulled out my phone, dialing Wyatt. "Is she there?" I asked as the other man answered.

"No. You find her?"

"No. Some kids picked on her, and she went running. I don't know where."

"Brooks?" Rory said into the phone, and I cursed.

"I'll find her, Rory. I promise."

"I'll search too. I don't know, just tell everyone. I'm sure she's fine. She's got to be fine."

I looked over my shoulder, and I was far enough away that I couldn't hear what they were saying, but I saw Rory and Cameron running out of the building, the other Wilders moving in a quick unit.

Trace came running up to me as I searched through the field, down the embankment where we had acreage of land that was open space that was off limits to guests. There were coyotes, rocks, places to fall, cacti, and countless other areas that were roped off for a reason.

"Okay, what is she wearing?" Trace asked.

I shook my head and then froze. "Jeans, pink sneakers, a white T-shirt with little pink daisies on it, and pigtails."

I couldn't quite believe that I remembered everything about what the little girl had been wearing, but we had all had breakfast that morning, even Cameron.

It was as if we had been a family. And I'd be damned if I lost that kid.

"On it. You keep this way, keep your phone handy. And we'll canvas the area. I'm sure she's just behind a little building or something, okay?"

"Yeah, yeah," I bit out, my voice short, and then I was running over the hill and down past the rocky ledge where any number of accidents could happen.

Bile filled my throat, but I kept going, calling out for Alice. "Alice! It's Brooks. Where are you?"

Nothing. Then my phone buzzed.

Heart racing, I answered. "Do you have her?"

"No. Do you?" Rory asked, and I heard the panic in her tone. And yet, she wasn't crying or shouting, and I knew she was being strong for Cameron.

"No, but we will. I'm searching, and I hear the others searching too."

"Okay. We'll find her. Please find her, Brooks," Rory whispered.

"I will," I promised.

And I hung up, sliding my phone into my back pocket as I continued to search.

There was a large crest of limestone, some of it had fallen in thanks to erosion over time, and a huge cactus was right next to it. I either had to walk over the limestone or take the long way around, but I had a feeling the limestone was too weak to handle my weight, so I jogged past the cactus when the sound of a little sob hit me.

I kept running, cursing as one of the barbs stuck into my arm. But I ignored the pain as I finally saw a little girl cowering underneath a copse of small oak saplings that hadn't fully grown yet and jagged limestone pieces. She had a cut on her knee, and one pigtail had fallen out, yet it was all I could do not to run to her and pick her up into my arms.

"Are you okay?" I asked, my voice shaky.

Alice put her arms around my neck, holding tightly enough that I nearly couldn't breathe.

"Brooks. I got lost. And then there was a cactus."

I looked down at her knee, at the two little barbs sticking out of it, and I shifted her weight so that I was cradling her in my arms.

"We'll take care of that as soon as we get a Band-Aid, okay?"

She nodded, tears streaking down her dirt-stained cheeks.

I had gotten barbs like that in my knee once when I was a kid, and pulling it out wasn't easy because of the hooks, hence why I hadn't bothered with the ones in my arm. We would just deal with it, but all that mattered was Alice was safe.

I moved past the pile of rocks and saw Ridge running towards me.

The look of relief on my brother's face nearly knocked me to my knees, and he pulled out his phone.

"Brooks has got her," he said, and I realized I hadn't called anyone. I had just held this little girl and knew I needed to get her to Rory.

Because, damn it, I loved this family. With everything that I had. And, as Rory and Cameron ran towards us, and we held each other close, it was all I could do to hold them even tighter or run away.

And the scary thing is, I didn't know what the answer should have been.

CHAPTER TWELVE
RORY

"Thank you for saving my sister," Cameron whispered, and I leaned against the doorway, watching as Cameron wrapped her arms around Brooks's waist. The man I had slowly fallen in love with, without even trying, held her close, his shoulders tense.

"She would have found her way back up. But don't worry. We found her. So many people were looking for your sister. You guys are never alone. Do you understand that? You have been adopted by the Wilders. We sort of take over."

I ran my hand over my heart, watching as Cameron's eyes widened and a small smile played on her face.

I'd rarely watched that little girl smile, as she didn't

do it for me. But if Brooks could do it, I would take that as something.

I let out a breath, watching as the two talked about soccer, of all things, and I made a note to sign Cameron up for a local team. She hadn't told me a thing, said she wanted to do nothing, but, if she and Brooks could talk about it, maybe it was something I could help with at least quietly.

Alice came out of the bathroom, all spick and span from her bath, and I lifted my arm so she could slide next to me.

"My knee doesn't hurt, which is nice. But Brooks said it might hurt later."

"As I, too, have been hurt by a barb from a cactus before, I can tell you it might hurt in a bit. But don't worry, we will keep an eye on it, okay?"

"Does Brooks have an owie too?"

"I'm all good, Alice. Don't worry," Brooks said as he lifted his arm.

Alice looked up at me then, and my heart caught. Because that was my sister's smile. My smile.

Every once in a while, it was like a two-ton truck to the chest, reminding me that my twin was gone.

I hadn't had peace to grieve. To realize that the person that I had thought would be with me until the end of time, my other half, would be out of my life forever.

First by choice, then by fate.

But as I watched Alice scramble onto the couch next to Brooks, the three of them with their heads bent together as they looked at something on his tablet, I couldn't help but stare and wonder at the fact that part of my sister was here.

And I had almost lost one of them.

Emotionally, I had almost lost the other. But Cameron smiled at me softly before going back to look at whatever Brooks had in his hands, and maybe, just maybe, I could figure this out.

"What are guys looking at?" I asked, clearing my throat.

Cameron looked up at me, her gaze going wooden, but didn't say anything. Alice grinned. "We're looking at different soccer teams to pick our favorite local one."

I raised a brow at Brooks, who gestured for me to sit on the other side of Alice.

I sank onto the couch cushion and took the throw off the edge, wrapping it around the four of us. Cameron didn't push away, nor did she look at me.

Was it because she saw her mother? Or was it because she just didn't like me. I was going to give her a little more time, and then we would get to the root of it. Because this was it. This was our family. The three of us. And I couldn't fix it. Of course, it wasn't just the three of us on this couch. And that was something I was going to have to make a decision about soon. But for now, I leaned against Alice and looked at the teams on the screen. "We don't have a local team?" I asked.

"No, there's one in Austin and Houston, at least in this league for women. There's a men's team, but I have a feeling we want to become fans of a woman's team?" he asked.

"Duh."

"Cameron," I warned.

She sighed. "I mean, yes. We need to figure out what the team colors are and everything. I want to know more."

"We can make that happen," I said, my heart beating quickly in my chest. Because Cameron was interested in something other than glaring at me. The day was a miracle of all miracles. My family was safe, and Cameron was looking at something for the future. And Brooks was underneath my roof.

My heart raced a little bit more at that.

"Okay, so who is our team?"

"Well, I'm in Austin more often than not, and tickets are a little easier to get."

I glared at him. "I don't know if tickets are in our budget," I whispered.

"Not season tickets," he said with a shake of his head. "But you know, a couple of tickets for me and my brothers."

Cameron gave him a look, and he grinned. "And maybe as rewards for good behavior, doing your chores, getting grades that make you proud, or I don't know because it's a day that ends in Y."

I wanted to glare at him, but I couldn't. I just looked at the way that he made Cameron smile, and I couldn't help but smile the same. The damn Wilder men were dangerous.

I looked at my phone, and my eyes widened. "Okay, I didn't realize how late it was."

"It took us a little while to get home from the Wilder Retreat," he said softly.

Yes, because everybody had needed to make sure that Alice was okay, and then, of course, an actual wedding had to take place. The bride and groom hadn't been aware that a little girl had been lost for twenty minutes and that my world had nearly ended once again.

"Well, I like the team colors. Because I like purple."

"Purple's nice. And I like the team colors too," Cameron said shyly.

"Good. I guess we'll have to do our research. I only know football, a little bit of hockey, and women's rugby," he said with a grin.

"Should I ask about the women's rugby?" I asked dryly.

"You know exactly why we know about women's rugby," he added just as dry.

I snorted before I pulled myself off the couch, and we went to tuck the girls in. Brooks read another story as I held Cameron close, and she didn't pull away this time. And it started to feel like a routine.

That scared me a bit, though, because Brooks and I definitely hadn't discussed anything like a routine. Because if he needed to back away because it was too hard or something he didn't want, he wasn't just going to break my heart. He was going to hurt these two little girls that I loved more than anything.

So maybe we needed to have that big talk. But not right now.

Not at this moment.

As we found ourselves in my bedroom soon after with the door closed, I sank on the edge of the bed and rolled my shoulders back. I looked down at my hands and sighed. No matter how many times I had washed them today, there was still dirt under my fingernails, and I probably needed that same shower that Alice had taken. Because I had run down that embankment just like Brooks had, clinging to my family.

"I can't believe I lost her," I said after a moment.

Brooks had sat down in the reading chair in the corner, taking off his boots. "We all had an eye on her, and she knew better than to run out into the field like that."

"She's just a little kid. And she got scared and hurt because of something that those other kids said. I sometimes forget how cruel kids can be."

"You live with Cameron and the way she speaks with you. I don't think you can truly forget."

I winced. "I don't know how to fix that. I don't know if it's because she sees her mother in me or that she's so angry she needs to lash out. I'm just sick over it."

"I think it's a bit of both," Brooks said as he came forward. He cupped my cheek and ran his thumb over my lips.

"Let's go downstairs, watch a movie, have some Wilder Wine, and just relax, okay?"

I bit my lip and nodded, knowing we just needed a moment. While I wanted to get into bed and let myself forget while being in his arms, we didn't actually get to spend too much time alone. Funny, for a man that I couldn't get enough of, sometimes we didn't have time to just sit and talk without the girls or his family around.

"Do you mind if I bring my tablet? I probably should go through a few work things."

"As long as you don't mind me doing the same," he said with a laugh. "Maybe we let ourselves do that for half an hour and then relax?"

"Oh the joys of being self-employed. What do you mean you're supposed to take some time off?" I teased.

He slid his palm over my cheek and kissed me softly. I moaned into him, wanting more, and told myself that I needed to stop. I just needed to breathe.

"Come on, if we don't stop, I'm going to fuck you right at the edge of this bed, and then we're never going to get up."

"You say that like it's a bad thing," I teased.

"Minx," he growled before he bit my lip, a little harsher than usual, and kissed the sting away.

I pressed my thighs together, wondering exactly why that had been so damn hot.

I let him take my hand and lead me downstairs to the family room, where Brooks had set up a large couch and TV.

"Have I ever told you how much I love the furniture that you've chosen for this house?"

"What's funny is that I never used to be good at

that," he said as we sank down onto the cushions, wine in hand. As well as our tablets.

"What do you mean?" I asked, wondering what Brooks wasn't good at. It was a little annoying sometimes.

"When I first built the company, my job was to design the homes, but really, just do whatever jobs I could get. Whether it was carpentry, electric work, and even plumbing. I was certified in all of that and was trying to be the jack of all trades. In the end, though, I needed somebody to help me narrow it down and figure out exactly what I wanted. Instead of working seven days a week for fourteen-hour days, wondering why I had no life. I mean, I can put in an entire new bathroom in two days, except for the glass and any extra design work, but I couldn't actually make it a home."

"Amara. That was Amara's job, right?" I asked, wondering why I even had to say her name. Why bring up ghosts in a space that was already tentative. But that wasn't fair. It wasn't fair to Brooks, me, or Amara.

He smiled then, and it was such a soft smile that it was like a kick in the gut. Not because I was jealous. But because of the fact that she wasn't here anymore. This woman had loved Brooks, and he had loved her. She must have been amazing.

"She pretty much organized me. I didn't want to work for other people constantly and fall behind. Or be on too many jobs, so they ended up like shit, or be forced to cut corners. So I found good guys, trained them, and made sure that they were certified. But Amara was the one who kept us in line, and learned how to fit a space. She was better at picking the tile or other silicates we used, even the fixtures." He rolled his eyes. "I would do my best at figuring out what bathroom fixture would look the best for a bathroom, and then she would come by and point to something, and I realized that I was going down the wrong direction."

"Really? I can't picture you not knowing what you want."

"We both know that I sometimes tell myself what I want, and then I ignore what I really want," he whispered before we both smiled softly, and he continued.

"I know how to decorate a place now, maybe not with the right linens or extra touches, but I know how to set a stage because of her. And she knew how to change a light switch without electrocuting herself."

"That I cannot do," I teased.

"I can teach you. If you want. It's always good to be able to do a few things on your own, but it's also good to find a handyman who can do it for you."

"I guess it's good that if you're not sleeping next to me, you're right next door."

"That is true," he said with a laugh.

"But yes, I did an okay job with the furniture in here, and I think I'm learning a little bit more with each home."

"How many homes do you own?" I asked as I leaned against the back of the couch.

"Seven," he said quietly.

I nearly choked on my wine. "Seven?"

"Well, I've built eight on this piece of land, and while it's not a full neighborhood, eventually it's going to be, and then I'll have to deal with the laws on that. I'm not going to want to own all of the homes at that point."

"Are you going to make an HOA?"

"Please, don't even mention that phrase in this house."

I grinned. "You're like this scary landlord, aren't you?"

"Not really. If any of the renters want to buy, they're welcome to, but most of them are military and know they're going to leave in a couple of years."

And then everything clicked. "Just like your cousins."

"Exactly. They were in and out of places often, and I

know finding a good place to rent where you can trust the landlord isn't always easy. And having a little bit of space these days just doesn't happen. We're close enough to the base that they can go in if they need to or remote work. Either way, it's a good school district, and it's not like I'm collecting an evil amount of rent."

"No, you're just making sure people have a way to move quickly if needed."

"Exactly. Having to sell your home after living in it for two years because you got orders is a whole other set of paperwork that most people don't need. And the Wilders own this land. We might as well use it for something that will help others. And help my business."

I snorted. "There's always that."

"People need to eat."

"That is true. And I don't know when I'm ever going to be able to own a home." I looked down at the wine glass, realized I had drunk nearly all of it, and set it down. "I can't believe I just said that out loud."

"I thought you were trying to save before this. Before you moved in here?" he asked gently.

"I was, but I'm a small business owner that does graphic art. Getting the girls' medical insurance was a pain, and once I hit the new year, it's going to be even harder." My stomach ached at that thought.

"Do you qualify for anything?"

"Some. It's a whole process, and I'm grateful that Everett is decent at actually figuring all that out with me. But my small savings is dwindling down slowly when it comes to new shoes and upcoming sports and other things that they want to do. Let alone therapy and doctor's appointments, and one day the girls are going to need cars, and then there's prom dresses and college, and I can't even think about it all."

"Hey, hey, just breathe. We'll figure it out."

It was funny that he said we, because we weren't technically a we. This was nice, and I was so grateful that we had a roof over our heads, but I needed to remember that this could all be temporary. He could be temporary. But I didn't want to ruin the entire night, as we had already had a stressful day.

"I'm trying not to think too hard about everything that's coming, but I also have to be realistic. I'm so grateful that we have this place because I couldn't afford it otherwise."

"You never have to worry about a place to sleep, Rory. Ever."

I reached over and ran my hand over his jaw. He turned his head and kissed my palm, and another little slice slid into place, and I knew falling in love with him fully would be inevitable.

"I know that I need to stop worrying about every single thing in the future, and I will. Eventually. It just keeps me up at night sometimes."

He frowned, tangling his fingers with mine. "I hate that you even have to worry about that. That the girls didn't have savings or anything."

"No, they didn't. But we haven't heard a single thing from the people that my sister got involved with, and I guess that's worth it."

"You know I looked them up, right?"

I raised a brow. "What do you mean?"

"We looked them up. We wanted to make sure it wasn't going to be a problem later. But the whole community is actually quite peaceful. There's no violence or police investigations into them. There's literally nothing to connect them to anything illegal other than that hinky feeling you got."

I let out a breath. "Ava and I looked them up too. They're just insular, and I don't know, they wanted money, they got it, and I got the girls. Honestly, they're so far from my mind that they don't matter."

"They don't. But I still want to kick them."

"To be honest, even my lawyer looked at the funds. There wasn't much. My brother and sister were in debt, they didn't own their own home, and there wasn't much in their savings account. At least for the girls."

Brooks's eyes widened. "What?"

"There wasn't. I don't know why I thought there would be more, or at least something. But in the end, the girls are safe, and I'm going to do my best to make sure they have a safe future."

"You're a good aunt, Rory."

"I don't always feel like it. Alice... I think Alice is doing okay."

"She loves you."

"She loves you too," I blurted.

"Yeah, that kid has me wrapped around her finger. Hell, so does Cameron, even though I want to growl at her."

"Sometimes I need to growl at her too. But her therapist and I are working on it. One day, she's not going to roll her eyes at me. However, that day will probably be on her 13th birthday when she turns into a teenager, and suddenly, it'll be a whole new set of eye-rolling."

"You know, that's going to happen."

"I went from zero to teenager in a blink, and I'm kind of sad I didn't get the baby years."

"Did you ever want to be a mom?" he asked softly.

"Maybe. I mean, I always thought I would. Once I found the right guy." I quickly looked down at my tablet, trying not to meet his gaze at that.

"Amara and I had wanted kids, and then she got

sick, and kids didn't happen. But I figured I'd be a good dad. At least I'm a decent uncle with Faith, and I guess with my cousins' kids. They all call me uncle. It's a little too difficult to figure out family connections the other way."

I met his gaze then and leaned forward, brushing my lips against his.

"You're a great uncle, and you're amazing with the girls. Honestly, I don't know how I would be functioning right now without you or the Wilders."

"You make me happy, Rory," he said reverently.

My heart thudded in my chest. "Yeah?"

"Yes. I didn't realize how unhappy I was, even if I thought I was doing okay. So thank you, for making me happy."

I sighed into him as his lips brushed against mine. "I don't think we're going to get any work done," I teased.

"I don't think so either. Come on, let me take you to bed."

"I do like the sound of that."

"And then, one day, I'm going to actually take you out on a date."

I held both of our wine glasses as he took our tablets, and I frowned.

"What do you mean, we eat together often, you're

here most nights, I thought we were dating?" I asked, suddenly feeling awkward.

"Rory, yes. I think we're beyond whatever the name is, considering how many nights I spend here. But I rarely get to actually take you out. Just the two of us."

"We went rollerskating with the girls."

"Yes, and had greasy chicken sandwiches and onion rings, and it was the best food I've had in a while as long as you don't tell Kendall that."

I snorted. "I promise."

"And we went to that baseball game, and we eat at the Wilder Retreat often, and we do all of that, with the girls. And I think it's about time I spoil you. Just saying."

I smiled then and let him kiss me softly until my toes curled.

"Come on, let's get upstairs."

We set the wine glasses in the dishwasher, turned off the lights, and I let him carry me upstairs, knowing the girls were safe, and I was in the arms of the man who literally swept me off my feet.

Maybe, just maybe, I was doing this whole life thing right.

At least for now.

CHAPTER THIRTEEN
BROOKS

Sweat slicked down my back as I dug out the final post and set my shovel down so I could wipe away the dirt from my face.

I had spent all morning at the Austin site and now needed to fix this damn post for my fence because the heavy winds had knocked it out. It didn't matter that I had settled the whole thing with cement and had even used metal poles as the stationary posts between the wooden slats. When heavy winds that were near tornado strength hit you in South Texas, a fence or even parts of roofs couldn't last.

I needed to finish this up pretty quickly, so I could shower and get ready for the next phase of my plan.

A smile played on my lips, but I tried not to look too

satisfied because I wasn't the only one setting up this particular plan.

No, this time, I had help.

It was odd to think that I was sitting here, finishing up a few pieces of yard work on a home that I owned so I could kidnap the woman I was seriously falling for.

I paused, hand over my heart for an instant as I let those words sink in.

Amara had been the only woman I'd ever loved. And until the moment I had been forced to say goodbye, I thought she would be the only woman that I would ever love for the rest of my life. That hadn't been the case in the end. And despite the promise I had made to her saying I would try again, I wouldn't have thought I would have. And yet here I was, falling for Rory Thompson. She was secretive with her feelings, outgoing when she needed to be, and yet so scared about making mistakes where she could hurt those she loved that I couldn't help but want to be the person that she leaned into through the worst of it.

I was head over heels for her and had been for longer than I cared to admit.

Maybe there had been a reason she had been the first one I had let myself be with. And the person who had haunted my dreams even though I thought I would never see her again.

Now there was no escaping her. Not that I wanted to escape her.

"Brooks! Are you ready?"

I turned to see Alice running towards me, a smile bright on her face, and I looked behind her, hoping that nobody else had heard. She dashed through the open gate between the two homes, and I smiled. "I'm getting there. I have to shower first, though. Are you guys all set?"

"Yep." She looked over her shoulder and then tried to whisper, though it came out more of a shout.

"Ava and Faith are going to be over soon to watch us. And that means you can kidnap Aunt Rory."

My lips twitched. "That sounds like our plan. Is Cameron distracting her?" I asked, enjoying the fact that the girls were helping me with this.

I had been right before in which I had told Rory that we hadn't actually been out often. For two people who spent most nights together and were slowly figuring out the way that our lives could work, no matter what happened in the future, we didn't spend much time alone outside of our homes.

So tonight, I was going to try to make that happen.

Even if it felt as though I didn't know what I was doing completely.

"Okay, you go make sure that Cameron is

distracting your aunt, and then I will finish this up before I shower so I can take your aunt out. What do you think?"

"I think that's okay." She pouted her lips and tapped them with her pointer finger as if she were thinking hard. I did my best not to smile because the kid was too damn cute.

"Why are you fixing your fence now?" she asked softly.

Always inquisitive, I went back to work as I answered. "Because we're getting another windstorm over the next week, as well as possible dry lightning. So I want to make sure that there's nothing out here that could potentially hurt somebody in case the wind does pick up. I'm almost done, and then I will get ready. Tomorrow, I'll finish prepping the rest of the yard and land around us, just in case."

"What's dry lightning, and just in case of what?"

"Dry lightning is when there's a lightning storm without rain around here. Because we live near a lot of brush that could catch fire, we have to be careful. A lot of this area isn't developed, which is good for us, but we also want to make sure that the wildlife is safe, and if something does catch fire, it can't hurt us."

"I don't like that. It's scary."

"It's why I am spending a lot of time making sure

that we prepare and keep the area safe. It's okay, Alice. We've got this." I reached out and wiped a spare fleck of dirt off her face, only leaving more clay behind.

She giggled and smiled up at me with her newly gap-tooth smile since she had just lost a fresh baby tooth.

"Did the Tooth Fairy visit?" I asked, though I knew the answer.

"Yes. Aunt Rory was very excited to tell me all about the Tooth Fairy because they didn't get to visit my old house. But they like it here. It's like a home here." She smiled brightly, and I swallowed hard, that familiar kick in the gut whenever she spoke about her past, even if she didn't even realize what she was saying.

I didn't know exactly what Rory's twin had been doing before the girls had moved here, before everything had changed. But the girls were settling down and figuring out their lives. Yes, Cameron still sometimes lashed out at Rory, but it was out of pain more than anything. The fact that the girl was helping me set up this date tonight spoke more about her acceptance of her new life.

"If there is a fire, we'll be okay, right?"

I set my things down, knowing I'd have to put everything away in a moment. And then I held out my arms. Alice ran to me, and hugged me tightly, and I just ran my hand down her back.

"We are taking care of the land, so that way, the land takes care of us. I know you were scared when you were out in that field by the resort all alone, but you're not going to run away like that again, are you?"

"I promise."

"Good. Because we would be worried if you did. But don't worry okay? We're always going to be here."

"Not always. Mommy and Daddy weren't always."

I could have rightly kicked myself for saying those words. I, above most people, understood that sometimes, no matter how hard you wanted them to stay, people you loved couldn't always.

I kissed the top of Alice's head before I picked the little girl up and carried her back towards Rory's house.

"You're right. Sometimes life doesn't work out the way that you want it to, but your aunt and I are going to do our best to make sure that you guys are taken care of no matter what, okay?"

"Okay. But make sure that you have fun with Aunt Rory tonight. She deserves to be a princess."

I smiled at that. "Yes, she does." I kissed the top of her head again as I walked inside and set the little girl down. "Go distract your aunt while I go shower. And then, I'll be over to kidnap her."

"Okay!" she shouted before she ran upstairs to where presumably Cameron was asking Rory how to do makeup so that way Rory would be ready for our date tonight. The kid was slightly diabolical, and I loved it.

I ran back to my place, put everything back in the shed, and went into my house to shower. I was rarely at my place other than to grab a few things, and it didn't seem to bother the girls, so I wasn't going to let it bother me. I checked the weather map again, grateful it wasn't going to storm tonight. Fire wasn't the only thing that we worried about in these places, considering there was also wind damage like we'd already had, flash floods, and various other weather phenomena. But there was nothing we could do to stop it other than try to pick up the pieces if something else happened. It had just been a dry few months, and that meant if it did rain, flash floods were going to be an issue.

I shook my head, remembering the flash flood that almost killed somebody that we had loved in our family, but I pushed those thoughts from my mind and quickly slid on dark jeans, a button-up top, and figured that would have to be good enough. We weren't going fancy because Rory didn't like fancy, and I was grateful for that. A nice steak dinner, and then maybe making out in the back of my truck like we were teens again, was going to have to be a decent date.

I walked around the front of the house and knocked on the door, flowers in hand, wondering why I felt so damn nervous. It wasn't as if Rory and I were new at this, but it still felt pretty damn new.

"I've got it!" Cameron's voice called from the inside of the house, and my lips twitched as she opened the door. She had had on a full face of makeup but still looked her age. The glitter lip gloss helped.

"Oh good, you're here. She's all ready to go."

"I'm ready for what?" Rory asked as her eyes widened at the sight of me.

"What? What are you doing here."

"I'm kidnapping you, of course." I handed over the small bouquet to Cameron, whose eyes widened as Alice ran up.

"Do I get one too?" she asked.

"Alice," Rory muttered, but I just grinned.

"You do." I handed over the small bouquet to her before holding out the larger one for Rory.

"What do you think? I thought my girls could use some flowers."

"Brooks," she muttered as her eyes filled, taking the bouquet in her hands. She pressed the petals to her nose and inhaled.

"They're beautiful."

"Just Texas wildflowers. Nothing like roses, but I thought the girls could use a little color. What do you think?"

"I love them," Cameron said as she carefully played with one of the petals. "No one's ever given me flowers before."

My heart kicked, and I ran my hand carefully over Cameron's head.

"Well, now you have. Want to go put them in some water?"

"Okay! Oh, hi, Aunt Ava!" Cameron reached out and tugged at Rory's hand before the girls ran to the kitchen and they moved out of the way for Faith and Ava to walk in.

"What are you guys doing here? I'm so confused," Rory said as I held out my arms.

"Come here," I ordered, and she took a step forward without even thinking, and then she blushed as Ava threw her head back and laughed.

"He's kidnapping you, of course. And I'm here to play fun aunt. You look great, girl. I'm glad that Cameron had her way with you. Now, go. I've got the girls, and you guys are going to go have dinner. And have some fun."

"What kind of fun?" Faith asked, and Ava rolled her

eyes.

"Never you mind, Faith darling. Go see the girls in the kitchen. I'll be in right after you."

Faith ran off, and then she gave me a wink. "Be home late, I've got the girls. Have fun."

"I'm very confused. I thought we were just staying in?" Rory asked as she shook her head.

"I told you, it's time we actually leave the house more than once for a date. I'm sorry, you don't get a choice."

"You set all of this up?" she asked, her voice soft.

"Of course I did. Come on." I leaned forward and took her lips with mine. And she melted into me.

Ava let out a loud sigh before she literally shoved us out the door.

"Stay out late. The girls better be asleep when you get home." She winked, then pushed Rory's purse into her arms, and then closed the door in our faces.

Rory just looked at the closed door and then at me before she burst out laughing.

"Okay then. It seems like we're going out to dinner. I'm glad I put on shoes."

"Cameron was very strict in what she was planning on doing to get you ready," I said solemnly.

"That girl scares me, and I love her."

"She is pretty amazing. Come on, we have reservations at Twelve Oaks, and I hear a steak calling my name."

Rory's eyes widened. "Twelve Oaks? We're not going to one of the Wilder restaurants?"

"I think Kendall will be fine if we don't use one of her places. I thought it was time for me to take you out of the Wilders' reach and just the two of us."

"Brooks."

"Don't look at me like that, or we're not making it to dinner."

She rolled her eyes and put her hand in mine.

"How did you accomplish all of this?"

"With a lot of help," I said with a laugh, and I walked her to my truck, grateful that she had agreed so readily.

Because I was falling in love with Rory, and I wasn't sure what I would do if she needed to walk away now.

By the time we were full of steak and our conversations had turned to the latest movies we had seen on our way back to the house, I was happy, full, and horny as hell. Because Rory's dress slowly slid up as she crossed her legs in the front seat and I couldn't help but look at the sweet silk of her thighs and wonder what they would look like with my beard burn on them.

"If you don't stop looking at me like that, we're going to have a problem," she teased.

I cleared my throat. "I don't think I mind that problem," I said as I pulled off to a small clearing on my land, but one that I knew others couldn't really see.

"Where are we going?" she asked, and I just grinned.

"You'll see."

And when I turned off the engine, with the moonlight sliding through the windows, she turned to me, eyes wide.

"Brooks Wilder, what are you planning?"

"Well, I figured it's time that we see exactly what those thighs look like wrapped around my neck. It's been a while since I've had dessert, and I swear to God, if I don't have your pussy on my face in the next ten minutes, I'm going to scream."

And when she just smiled at me, I knew I had just fallen head over heels with the woman of my dreams.

Rory's eyes widened as I leaned forward and brushed my finger along her jaw. "Ava's got the girls all night. What do you say we take this moment just for us?"

"Really? That's the line you're going with?" she asked. I undid her seatbelt and then slid my hand up her thigh, over the side of her panties. Her mouth parted, and I smiled.

"Yes, that's the line I'm going with." And then I

leaned forward and captured her lips with mine. She groaned into me, and I used my thumb to slide over her mound, loving the heat I could already feel from there.

"Come on, I want you."

"Then take me."

She moved her body so her back pressed against the door and lifted one leg up, baring herself to me.

"Damn woman," I growled as I gripped the back of her neck and crushed my mouth to hers. The windows began to steam up, but I didn't care. I explored her mouth, even as her hands gently and then not so gently ran over my body. It was a tough fit, but luckily, I had a big enough truck that when I leaned down over the center console, I shoved her dress up and then her panties to the side.

"Brooks!"

I didn't look up. Instead, I licked over her cunt, loving the way that she arched her body towards me. With one hand keeping her legs spread, I used my other to play with her swollen folds.

"Look at you, all pink and swollen and ready for my touch. I can fucking scent your cream from here. Already wet, and I haven't even really touched you. Look at you, my dirty, bad girl. You want my cock, don't you? Or do you want my tongue?"

"I just want to come," she teased.

"I can make that happen. I need you to come on my face. What do you say? Can you do that?"

"I think the question is, can *you* do that?"

She held one of her knees up, baring herself for me, and the other hand she used to pluck at her nipples over her dress.

Groaning, I leaned down and lapped at her, spearing her with two fingers. She arched for me, the confines of the truck almost too tight, but I didn't care. Instead, I fucked her hard with my two fingers, sliding in and out so the wet noises of our sex filled the car rudely. I knew we might have to be quick because even though we were on private property, anybody could drive down, and I didn't care. I wanted them to see me claim this woman as my own, to see her come for me with my name on her lips. So when I continued to suck her down, loving the way that she practically melted on my tongue, I kept moving faster, quicker, until she finally came, her legs shaking. She drenched my face, dripping down my chin as I continued to suck at her, needing her taste. And when I sat up and wiped my chin, she blushed so prettily.

"Look at you, practically squirting on my face."

"Brooks."

"What? You're so fucking hot. I can't help it."

I leaned forward and kissed her, knowing she could

taste herself on my lips. And then I grunted as she shoved me back, and I laughed.

"What?"

"It's my turn now."

And then she was on me, her hands on my belt buckle as she quickly undid my pants. I shifted my body, pulling my cock out of my boxer briefs.

"That's it, I'm not going to come down that pretty mouth, not unless you want me to, because I need to be in that pussy of yours. What do you think?"

"I think you can do both," she teased before she opened her mouth wide and took me deep inside. With my piercings, we had to be careful, but over the past months we had figured out a routine. And she was damn good with that mouth of hers. I wrapped her hair around my fist and lifted my hips up, slowly, oh so slowly, inching down that throat of hers. She opened her mouth wide, relaxing her throat, and I went even deeper. When she didn't gag, I grinned.

"That's my girl."

And then one of her hands was on my balls, the other on my hip, and I was fucking her face, both of us groaning into the confines of the truck.

I tugged at her hair, my balls tightening. "I'm going to come, baby girl. You want me to come on those tits? To paint them and rub it in so you know you're marked by me? Or do you want my cum down your throat?"

In answer, she hummed along my length and continued to bob her head.

I groaned, and then I was coming, grunting her name as I spurted down her throat, and she swallowed every drop of me. Not nearly sated, I leaned back against the door, my body shaking as she lifted her head and wiped her mouth.

"Well then," she teased, and then I was on her again, needing her lips.

"I need you."

"Then take me."

I shook my head and pulled her over to my lap.

"Not in here. I need that ass of yours, and to make you comfortable, we're going to need to move."

Eyes wide, we scrambled out of the truck, and I caught her before she fell.

I searched in the center console, pulled out the lube and condoms, and both of us laughed as we went to the edge of the truck bed. I set down the tailgate, grateful that I got the truck that had the extender, and pulled down the side-step.

"Up you go," I teased and then she sat down at the edge of the truck.

"What do you mean, my ass?" she said deadpan.

"You know exactly what I meant."

I kissed her then, ramping us both up as she wrapped her legs around my waist, pulling me towards her.

Her panties were already in the truck bed, and my jeans were practically falling down my hips, but I didn't care. I just needed her touch, needed her.

"That's it, you're so fucking beautiful," I whispered.

"You say that, and all you have is the moonlight to see me."

"Then take my word for it." I pulled her down off the truck bed slightly so she was on the side-step and flipped her over.

"Now, let me see that ass of yours."

I went down to my knees behind her, spread her cheeks, and licked and sucked. She groaned, pushing her ass back to my face as I ate her out, licking and then using my tongue to probe her asshole.

"So fucking beautiful."

I used the lube on two fingers, gently probing her ass as she groaned, tilting her hips up.

"So eager." I gently stretched her with one finger, then the second.

"That's it, just press back and relax," I whispered as she hissed out a breath.

"Brooks, you're too big," she whispered.

I pushed up her dress some more and kissed up her spine, licking at that, too, since I loved it so much.

"You tell me when to stop, I'm never going to hurt you, Rory. Believe me."

She looked over her shoulder then, and the moonlight glinted off her eyes.

"I trust you," she whispered.

And it was like a kick in the chest, and I nodded tightly, continuing to work in and out of her. I used my other hand to wrap around her waist, sliding my fingers over her clit, as she groaned.

And then finally she came again, pressing that sweet ass against my hand.

"Are you ready for me?" I asked, and she nodded.

"For you? Anything."

Undone, I positioned myself at her back entrance, my lube-covered condom ready to go.

"Now let out a deep breath, and push back as I go inside, okay?"

"Okay," she whispered.

And so I moved forward, the tight ring of her ass squeezing my cock so hard I knew I was going to come pretty quickly.

Slowly, oh so slowly, I worked my way inside as she pressed against me, and then we both sat there, buried to the hilt as we shook.

"Are you okay?"

"I'm too full. So full. And I need you to move. Please, Brooks."

"Anything you want, baby. I promise." I leaned forward and captured her mouth as she tilted towards me, and then I moved. Slowly, so slowly that I knew if I went any faster, I could hurt her, but I would never hurt Rory. Not now, not ever.

She pressed against me as we rocked into one another, my orgasm rising with each passing movement. So I moved my fingers around, sliding over her clit again before spearing her pussy, needing her to come. She shot off like a rocket, clamping around my dick, and then I moved once, twice, coming once again, as I whispered her name against her back, both of us shaking.

Finally, I slid out of her before using the washcloth and a bottle of water I had brought with me and gently cleaned us both. And when I lifted her so she sat on the edge of the truck bed again, slightly, gingerly, I kissed her softly, exploring her mouth, letting my hands roam over her breasts and then over her pussy.

"Sore?" I asked.

"Yes, but just hold me?"

I nodded, my cock filling again. So I wasn't surprised when she wrapped her hand around the base of my cock, and gently guided me inside that sweet pussy of hers. This time no condom, but that was fine. We were safe, and all I wanted to do was feel her around me.

I hadn't come this much in such a short period of time since I had been a teen, but this was all Rory. But instead of hard and fast, we just rocked against each other, letting the moonlight dance over our skin, as I took her mouth and rode each other to completion.

And I just held her, knowing I was never going to let her go.

I had tried to walk away from her before, not once, but at least twice. And I was never doing it again.

Soon I'd find a way to tell her. That she was mine and she was just going to have to deal with it. That I was going to be a damn Neanderthal and claim her in front of the rest of the world.

Because I loved Rory Thompson.

And now I just needed to make sure she knew that. Because I was never letting her go. No matter what came next.

CHAPTER FOURTEEN
RORY

The next day, everything ached, but it was a good day.

Something had changed the night before, and it wasn't just all of the dirty, inexplicably amazing things that Brooks and I had done in the back of that truck. My skin heated as I remembered, and I hoped nobody could read my mind. Because nobody needed those thoughts. Not even my best friend.

My lips curved into a smile as I thought about exactly how Brooks had cleaned us both up and cared for me in such an indescribably sweet way that it had brought tears to my eyes. But in the end, it was all I could do not to fall into a heap or at least melt into a puddle when I thought about him.

Because I loved him, and I hoped to hell that I would soon have the courage to tell him.

He had gone out of his way to make sure that we had an incredible night of just the two of us. And the girls had not only been taken care of, but they had been part of the planning.

The girls loved me. Or at least, liked me. They had helped Brooks ensure we had all had an amazing night. And we had crept into the house, underneath Ava's knowing gaze. Ava had slept in the guest room, while Faith had slept in Alice's trundle bed, and Brooks and I had huddled underneath my comforter. The only reason that Ava hadn't gone home was that Wyatt had been out of town and had just come back today after a distillery retreat. So now, the three of them were at the house for an early dinner, and we were going through class projects, prepping for the upcoming soccer season, and I was just blessed.

I still wasn't sure exactly how this had happened, though.

"You've been doing great with the new fence. You should come over and fix ours," Wyatt said as he pointed his beer toward Brooks.

Brooks stood at the grill and rolled his eyes. "You're an adult. You can do that yourself."

"But you're the handy one. I'm just the brains."

"Babe, if you're trying to get your brother to do something, maybe don't lie about the whole brain thing."

Wyatt growled at his wife and then chased her around the backyard, much to the delight of Alice and Faith, who ran around with them.

I shook my head, smiling at their antics and trying my best to ignore the flutters in my belly as I watched them move.

Once again, I knew I was a goner when it came to Brooks Wilder, and I was going to have to try to find a way to let him know. Without giving up everything.

Because I was so damn afraid that we were going too fast. That maybe he didn't think the same as me, or if I said something silly, I would ruin everything for me and the girls.

I had never been in love before, after all. I didn't know what I was supposed to be feeling or thinking.

"Is he going to put cheese on my burger?" Cameron asked, and I shook myself out of my thoughts and looked down at my niece. "You asked for it, and Brooks said he would. But maybe you should go double-check. We can walk over together."

Cameron wrapped her arms around her belly and shook her head. "No. It's okay."

I frowned and tugged her into the alcove where the others couldn't hear.

"Are you feeling okay? You look a little pale." I reached out and put my hand over her forehead. She flinched, but I didn't feel any heat.

"I'm fine," she grumbled.

"Cameron. What's wrong?"

"Everything's fine. I just... I don't want to talk about it." And with that, she stomped over to Brooks but smiled wide like she didn't have a care in the world.

I shook my head, wondering exactly what that was about.

Some days, I felt like the two of us had found our path; other days, I felt as if I was once again making a mistake.

She was so kind to me sometimes, and other times, pushed me away for no other reason than she knew I would come back.

Her 13th birthday was coming up, and I was already dreading the full teenage years. Twelve years old was already breaking me. I could not imagine the rest.

We all were in Brooks's backyard since he had the largest deck and grill, and as the wind picked up slightly, I pushed my hair back from my face and glared at the clouds off in the distance.

"Hey, do you think we should bring this party inside?" I asked as I pointed towards the clouds.

He scowled at them and shook his head. "They're going in the opposite direction, but you're right. The wind is picking up. We'll eat inside, but we should be okay for now for actually finishing up on the grill." He wrapped his arm around my waist and kissed me softly.

Wyatt whistled as the two youngest girls clapped their hands.

I rolled my eyes but blushed.

"Brooks."

"What? It's not like they don't know."

"Oh, we know," Cameron said, even as her lips twitched into a smile.

I grinned and leaned into him. "I don't want to know what you know."

She just laughed and went over to help Ava move a few things into the house.

I smiled and watched as the youngest girls danced around, and everything just felt right.

Like this was a family.

I missed my sister and my parents something fierce, but I also knew they were never coming back. We had somehow been forced to make this new family of ours, and while I couldn't say we were always blessed, not with the pain that brought us here, but with what we had right then? I wasn't going to take this for granted. Because the girls were healthy and they were safe, and the man I had fallen in love with had his arms around me.

Honestly, that didn't sound like too bad of a way to celebrate the end of a lovely weekend.

"Hey, are we eating at your place or at his," Ava asked, and I pulled myself out of my thoughts and grinned.

"I actually have some of the side dishes over at mine, so let's bring everything in there?" I asked.

"No problem. We're good here. Let me just..." Her voice trailed off as the hairs on the back of my neck rose. I turned to see what he was looking at, what had just made his face pale, and it felt like everything tilted on its axis.

An older couple stood there, both of them holding onto one another as they looked surprised to see Brooks here at his own home.

The husband had a stern expression on his face, and the woman was just staring at Brooks as if she were seeing a ghost. For some reason, I felt as though I needed to stand in front of him to protect him or hide so no one could get hurt.

"Brooks?" I asked, my voice soft.

"I— it's my in-laws," he whispered, his voice

broken. "I just, hey Wyatt, can you handle the grill? I'll be right back."

His brother gave him an odd look, pity filling his gaze as he looked at me before he gave me a tight nod.

"No problem. You guys head into the house, Brooks, you let me know if you need anything."

"Yeah. Yeah." Brooks squeezed my hand but didn't kiss me as he walked away without saying another word. He just left. Left us behind without looking back.

Luckily, I didn't think the girls quite understood what was happening as they had already been moving towards the house, but Wyatt did.

"Hey. We didn't know they were coming. It was a surprise. Everything's going to be okay. All right?"

"Yeah," I said, clearing my throat. "We're all good. I just hope Brooks is okay."

He gave me an odd look, but I didn't want to stay to interpret it. Instead, I took the last few things, other than the burgers themselves, back into my home, leaving Brooks back at his place with his in-laws and the slap in the face of a past that I knew still haunted him every time he closed his eyes.

I just had to hope he was okay. I wanted to wrap him in my arms and tell him that he was okay. That he didn't have to worry about me, that I would take care of him. And yet, part of me didn't know if I had the right.

How silly was that? I was just telling myself that I was in love with him, that I needed to tell him, and the parents of the woman that he had loved more than anything, the woman that had shaped him into the man that he was now, had made him look as if he had seen a ghost.

The ghost that had always stood between us, or perhaps, next to us.

I shook myself from those thoughts, knowing they weren't going to help anyone, as I went to help a curious Ava set up the rest of the meal.

I looked over the crew, realizing that Wyatt had come in with the burgers to help set everything up with Ava. Faith and Alice played a game beside her, but I couldn't find Cameron.

The wind picked up, slamming open the back door that I hadn't latched properly, and I went to close it, only to see that Cameron was still outside.

"I'll be right back," I said, pushing my hair back from my face as the wind shoved it forward.

"Be careful out there, I think the lightning is coming pretty close."

Even as Wyatt spoke, an arc of lightning cracked over the sky, and I cursed.

"Cameron!" I called out.

But she didn't seem to hear. Instead, she kept walking towards the field, and my pulse raced.

"Cameron!"

I ran past the gate and towards the little girl that I loved with all my heart and reached for her. She whirled away from me, and my eyes widened.

"What's wrong, baby?"

"Everything's wrong. Mom's not here. She promised she would be here for this."

I blinked at the venom in her tone, wondering where it had come from.

"For what, baby? You know she would've been here if she could. What's wrong?"

"Today's the day that Mom said I'd be a woman, and yet she's not here. She promised she would help me. And I don't know what I'm doing."

It all clicked then, the mood swings, the paleness of her face earlier.

"Oh, baby. You started your period?" I asked softly.

"Yes. And I don't know what I'm doing. I know Mom talked about it, and so did the school, but it's stupid. Why do I have to do this?"

I shook my head even as I reached for her. "It is stupid. I hate that it's every month. But you're not alone in this. I'm here. Let's talk about it."

"Every month?" she asked, eyes wide. "I don't want to do this every month."

"It's not fair that not everybody has to deal with this for sure. But we'll handle it. Let's get you back home and taken care of. Maybe get you something to drink and some Ibuprofen? You think that will help?"

"I don't know. I just want it to stop. Because Mom promised she would be here, and she's not. She had to go off and die because she and Dad wanted a weekend alone. And I hate that she's gone. I hate her."

"Oh, Cameron. You don't hate her. You can hate everything that's happened, but you don't hate your mother."

"You don't know what I feel. She was supposed to be here. She was supposed to help me with this. And I love you. I know that you're great, and I hate the fact that I keep yelling at you. But I can't seem to stop. Every time that I want to say something right, it comes out wrong, and then I'm a bitch. And I don't want to be a bitch. Mom would hate me being mean to you. Because you have her face. You're just like Mom, but you're not. And I just want my mom." She burst out into tears then, as the wind continued to ramp up around us. I pulled her into my arms, even though she tried to tug away.

"It's okay. No, actually, I'm wrong. Nothing's okay.

But I love you. We all love you. Your mom still loves you. I know that she's not here, and I miss my sister every single day. But she wouldn't want us to yell at each other or to feel bad that we miss her. So let's get inside before it starts raining, and let me take care of you all, okay? I know I'm not your mom, but I am your aunt. So let me love you like your aunt, okay?"

"I miss my mom. But I love you too."

My heart swelled as I held her close.

"I love you so much, kid." Tears slid down my cheeks as Cameron cried in my arms.

Lightning cracked again and then two more times in rapid succession.

Shivering, I looked up and realized that the storm was now overhead, and the lightning was far too close. My hair stood on end again, but this time, it had nothing to do with Brooks's in-laws.

"We need to get inside, Cameron. Now," I said, and she must have heard the urgency in my tone.

Cameron looked up and nodded as another arc of lightning slammed into the breaker near us.

I pulled at Cameron, running before the lightning even finished its arc, the breaker bursting into flames, and then everything seemed to happen at once.

Cameron screamed, tripping over her feet. I tugged

her up, ignoring the tears streaming down her face and the blood on her knee.

"We need to get going," I called, knowing we were too far away from the house for anyone to hear us over the lightning and wind.

But the smell of smoke hit my nostrils, and then the fear set in.

Because there was no rain, only lightning and fire.

And as I coughed, Cameron doing the same, I pulled her close and skidded to a halt as the fire surrounded us.

"Aunt Rory!" Cameron called.

"It's okay. We'll be okay," I lied. "There's a gap over there. We'll get through, and I'm sure the others are on their way and called the fire department. Just keep your head down and stay close. I've got you, Cameron. I am *not* letting you go. Ever."

The fear in her gaze didn't subside but she nodded, the trust in her eyes nearly sending me to my knees. And now I had to pray to whatever gods were listening that I hadn't truly lied to my niece about everything.

Because the others couldn't see us, and the fire had spread far too quickly.

And the only thing I could think of as I pulled Cameron close, keeping her face away from the flames, was Brooks, and hoping to hell he'd find us. I refused to let the man I love lose anyone else, nor would I let Cameron get hurt.

So we did the only thing we could.

We ran toward the edge of the flames... and prayed.

CHAPTER FIFTEEN
BROOKS

I stared at Erin and Bo, wondering what I was supposed to say in the situation. It had been a couple of years since I had seen Amara's parents, and while I wasn't displeased to see them, I was still shocked.

"Bo, Erin, can I get you guys something to drink? Coffee? Tea?"

Erin shook her head as she looked past me, her eyes narrowed.

"No, we're fine. We're staying at a hotel downtown because we just needed a trip out, just to get out of our city. Sorry, we didn't call ahead." Bo frowned. "I see we should have."

The censure in his tone wasn't lost on me, but it had been over four years now since Amara had died, and I didn't know the right number of years to mourn, the appropriate time it was to move on. Because grief wasn't static. Nor did the phrase 'move on' make sense. Because you weren't leaving anyone behind. You were just a different person.

"I'm glad you're getting out. Though it's a bit of a stormy day, not quite good for touristy things."

"I see you're having a barbecue," Erin said, her voice clipped.

I looked at the woman who had cried in my arms when we had finally said goodbye to Amara and then slammed her fists into my chest because I allowed my wife to sign a DNR. Bo had understood, had calmed his own wife down, but things had been strained in the past few years. It wasn't that we disliked each other. It was just awkward to be in a place where the one person that connected us was no longer here. And I didn't need them, and they didn't need me.

Which was a sad state of affairs.

"My brother, his wife, his kids, and my friends were here. Before the storm came in, it was a good day for a barbecue. We made extra. You're welcome to stay." I paused. "We would like you to stay." It was honest too. I didn't resent them. How could I? They had given me one of the most special people of my life. Their daughter. I wasn't going to resent them. I couldn't.

I just had to navigate these murky waters I had never expected.

"Oh, I don't know if we should," Erin said after a moment before she let out a breath and set down her bag. "We should have called. I'm just not good at this, Brooks. You were our son, and then the world changed, and I don't know how to talk to you without bringing back all of those memories."

I swallowed hard and did the one thing that I knew how to do. I moved forward and took her hand, trying not to break in the process.

"You don't have to say were... If you want, I will always be your son. Amara didn't choose to go just as much as we didn't choose to let her go." Bo let out a shaky breath next to me, but I continued. "I love your daughter. I will always love her. But I made a promise to her, one that has taken a long time for me to truly realize what that promise meant."

"What are you talking about, Brooks?" Bo asked, his gaze intent.

And as I let out a breath, I told them of a promise I had made their daughter. One that had slowly broken me before I had realized what exactly it had meant.

Tears streamed freely down Erin's face, but she nodded solemnly. "That was our daughter. Too good for all of us."

I let out a rough chuckle. "Believe me, I know that. Amara was a better person than I ever was. I'd like to say I would've done the same thing. Asked her to move on so she wouldn't be alone, but I'm a selfish bastard."

Bo barked out a laugh at my curse, but Erin just grinned. "Frankly, so are we. Because we would do anything to get our daughter back. I think that's why we stayed away so long. Because I'm not good at this, Brooks."

"I don't think you're supposed to get good about grieving. About figuring out who you are now. But you're welcome to stay for dinner. Hell, you're welcome to stay here at my place if you don't want to go back to the hotel. Especially because it looks like it may, hopefully, rain soon."

Lightning crashed through the room, and we each jumped.

"That sounded pretty close," Bo said, and I nodded.

"Too close," I said, looking off into the distance. Everybody should be safe inside Rory's house, but I was still worried.

"Who was that woman?" Erin asked, and I looked towards the woman who had raised Amara, unable to read her face. That was usually the problem with Amara's mother. Because I couldn't read her usually. It wasn't that she was judgmental or mean; it was that she was hurting. And wanted others to hurt too. Not out of callousness but because she needed others to feel her pain. So she would lash out at those she knew could take it, meaning I wasn't going to let her do the same to the woman that I loved.

"That's Rory. The woman that I'm seeing. Those girls are her nieces. She's raising them after her sister and brother-in-law died earlier this year."

Erin put her hand over her heart, as Bo let out a grunt of pain.

"I wasn't sure how I was supposed to tell you. I don't want to hurt you. But I thought you should know the truth."

"Do you love her?" Erin asked, and I met the other woman's gaze, knowing lying wouldn't help.

"I do. I never thought I was allowed to. I thought that this would be it for me. Waiting until it was time for me to see Amara again. But that wasn't fair to her or me. So yes, I love Rory. Though I haven't told her yet, so if you guys could give me the grace of time for that, that would be wonderful."

"Oh, Brooks." Tears filled her eyes as she moved forward. I flinched when she cupped my face, but she just lowered her head and let out a breath. "I'm happy for you. And broken a little. But I'm happy. You took care of our daughter when we couldn't. When you were the only one she could hold because everything else hurt. You don't deserve to live in pain and loneliness for the rest of your life. I know I wasn't nice. And I have no excuse other than I was dying inside. But I really hope you're happy."

I looked over at Bo, who wasn't saying anything. Instead, he looked off into the distance, his jaw tight.

"We should head out before the storm truly hits. I don't even know why we came without warning you. I think we just got in the car, and then we were here."

"You're always welcome. Rory would say the same."

"Is she living with you?" Erin asked, her voice slightly clipped.

"She lives next door. The girls needed a place to stay when they lost everything, and well, it turned out for the best."

"Maybe one day we'll hear more. But—"

I turned at the look of alarm on her face and was running before I even thought twice.

"Call the fire department. Tell them that there's a brush fire. Quick."

"I'll do it right now. Oh my God, are there people out there?"

"I'm right behind you," Bo said, and I started running, my feet pounding on the deck stairs as I ran towards the sound of someone's scream.

Flashes of Amara's last words hit me, and I tried to push them out of my mind. I was not going to lose another person that I loved.

"Brooks! Cameron and Rory are out there!" Wyatt yelled, and I nearly tripped over my feet.

"Keep the kids back, and start working on our fire precautions to keep the houses safe. Do what you can. I'm getting the girls."

"I'm coming with you," Bo shouted as he ran right beside me, keeping up far more than I thought he would.

I knew he had his own demons by running with me, but we kept going.

Fire licked across in a straight line, the transformer that must have blown bursting once again into flames.

I searched for that familiar blonde hair, and all I could see were the flames, but the sound of someone's shout finally hit me.

"Rory!"

"Brooks! We're over here! We're cut off!"

"Damn it," I said, as I pulled off the flannel I had put on earlier, as the wind had picked up, and covered my mouth with it.

"I'll go get Wyatt and the hose. Or something. Don't run into those flames, Brooks!" Bo yelled.

"I'm not leaving them."

And without another word, I ran towards the edge of the flames, searching for a way through.

Finally, there was a slight gap, and I jumped over the line, ignoring the singe on my arm where the fire had gotten too close.

Bo shouted my name, and then Wyatt was there, but I didn't know what they were doing. Instead, all I could see was Rory huddled over Cameron, dragging the little girl towards where there was another break, but it was too far away.

"Rory!"

And then she turned towards me, eyes wide.

"No, you're going to get hurt!" she said, her hands shaking, but I didn't care. I just ran towards them and crushed them to me.

Without another word, I pulled Cameron into my arms and began to drag them towards the now-shortening break in the fire line. "We have to get there quick. Run."

"I'm scared!" Cameron yelled.

"I've got you. You guys are fine," I lied, but it didn't matter. I was going to get them out of this.

There was no fucking way I was going to let my family get hurt.

"Brooks, you're bleeding!" Cameron said, and as Rory cursed under her breath, we kept going.

Smoke billowed towards us, and I coughed, covering Cameron's head with my flannel, pushing the girls faster.

Another shock of lightning arced across the sky, but we ignored it, focusing single-mindedly on getting out of this fire. The field wasn't that big, and we were running out of room. Just as I feared the worst, the first drop of rain hit. Heat slammed into us as the fire came closer, and I pulled the girls behind me, but the rain finally broke, lashing through the flames and over our faces. I held Cameron's shaking body as I looked at Rory, and she finally broke down, tears bursting from her.

"Oh my God. Brooks."

"It's okay, the fire's down. It's going down," I said, hoping to hell that I wasn't lying. Even as the rain began to pour, Rory and I pulled the flannel off of Cameron's face. We searched for cuts or bruises, but she just shook her head and clung to both of us.

"I'm sorry. I love you. I love you both. Please don't be mad."

"We're not mad. We love you too, baby girl," Rory whispered as she clung to her niece, and I held them both close.

Out of the corner of my eye, I saw Wyatt, Bo, and

the others running toward us, and from what I could tell, even the kids were running toward us too.

I wanted to tell them to stay back, but the flames had receded, and as I stood there with most of my family in my arms, my knees nearly gave out.

"I love you," I whispered as I looked at Rory and hugged her tight.

"I love you too. I knew you'd come," she said as she sniffed. "I was going to get us out of there, I swear, Cameron, but I'm really glad you came, Brooks."

"I knew you'd come too," Cameron whispered through tears, and then my brother was there, cursing as he looked at my arm, but I gave him a look to tell him to ignore it. And then, when Alice ran towards us, leaping in the air, I caught her, ignoring the pain in my arm, and held my family close to me.

I let out a shake breath. "I love you, Rory. Forever."

She kissed my neck, holding onto the girls with me. "Same. I freaking love you so much. I'm really glad it's raining."

"Never do that again," Alice yelled, and I wanted to laugh, but instead, I tightened my hold as my in-laws watched on, and Wyatt had his arms around Ava and Faith, gesturing to the fire department for where to come and put out any additional flames.

Soot made me cough, and my arm hurt like a bitch,

but I kept my attention on the three women who had taken over my life and tried not to pass out.

Later, with my arm bandaged and my feet up on the coffee table, I watched from afar as Erin and Bo worked with Ava and the rest of my family, who had all come en force to my house, work on dinner.

Alice slept at the corner of the couch, one of my blankets over her, as Cameron played with her hair while the little girl slept.

And I sat with Rory leaning into me, my life sitting on this couch.

"I was scared, but I knew you'd come. Probably silly, but maybe not."

"I was always going to find you. That much I can promise you. I love you, Rory. I was just trying to figure out how to tell you. Next time, let's not let a fire do that."

"Deal. Because I love you too."

"Does this mean you're my Uncle Brooks now?" Cameron asked, her eyes puffy, but that smirk on her face told me she was trying to be brave.

"If that's what you like. But that does mean you have to listen to me when I tell you to do things."

"Fine," she said with a smile and a roll of her eyes, and she went back to braiding Alice's hair.

And I sat there with Rory in my arms, grateful that

she had come to the Retreat that day and I had seen her, knowing my life would be changed forever.

I just had never realized how much it would change.

Because I had been given a second chance, a chance to grow with this family of our own making.

And I knew some of the hardest days might be in front of us, but I wasn't going to take this for granted, not again.

I smiled over at my in-laws, who smiled back softly, each of them working on a different part of our dinner prep, and I figured that I was a very grateful man.

Then I looked up to the ceiling and closed my eyes, saying thank you to the woman who had made me promise something I never thought I would actually achieve.

Because grief really changed in every instant of breath and movement and time passing.

And your heart could grow over time. There wasn't space for merely one person. Instead it grew as you did, changed as you did. Because I loved Rory. And I would always love her. And in a way, the first woman I had ever loved had found a way to gift me the woman I loved now.

And maybe others wouldn't understand, but I didn't care.

Because I wasn't going to take this for granted. Not again. Not ever.

"So does this mean you're actually going to take a day off and heal?" Rory asked.

"Maybe," I said.

"Yes, he will," my eldest brother said, and I just nodded, knowing that the Wilders didn't back down easily.

I may have been the first Wilder to settle down, but now I was the final one to start over.

And that meant I was the final one to figure out exactly where it had all gone wrong and where it should have gone right.

And that meant I was never letting Rory go.

No matter how hard we had tried to ignore what had been there all along.

CHAPTER SIXTEEN
BROOKS

Tile bit into my knees as water slicked down my back, but I didn't care. Instead, I lifted Rory's leg up over my shoulder and used my other hand to keep her thighs steady as I pressed her against the shower wall.

"We're going to be late," she panted.

"Then you better let me have my breakfast."

"Brooks," she gasped as I leaned forward and lapped at her cunt. She tasted of honey and sweetness, and I couldn't help but explore, knowing that this could be every morning and it wouldn't matter. Because this was our future. The woman that I loved, with her legs wrapped around my shoulders, as I ate my fill. I sucked at her clit as she arched in front of me, and I was grateful that I had built this shower to have a slight ledge. That way, she could lean against it and not slide down.

"Brooks," she panted again.

"That's it, say my name," I breathed against her pussy, as I speared her with two fingers, curling them to get that sweet bundle of nerves. She came then, clamping around my fingers as she rocked her hips on my hand.

"That's good. Keep getting yourself off. Rock those hips. Show me exactly what you want."

She met my gaze then, continuing to move her hips as she came down from her orgasm.

"That's it. That's my good girl." I kissed her pussy once more before removing my fingers and standing up.

"Open," I demanded, and I slid my fingers between her pouting lips as she obeyed what I said.

"Taste yourself. Do you like that? That's what I want every morning. This taste on my tongue."

She licked at my fingers before I removed them from her mouth and kissed her with everything that I had. "I need you. Every morning. Right now. Please."

I smiled against her lips, nodding softly, before I lifted her leg once again, positioned myself at her entrance, and slid home. She groaned into me as I froze, letting her take her time to adjust to my size.

"I'm never going to get used to that," she whispered. "I mean, what a way to wake up," she teased.

I took her mouth again, sliding my fingers between us to rub over her clit.

"I don't want to get used to this. I want it to feel fresh and new every morning and then feel like home all at once. Because you're my home, Rory."

Tears slid down her cheeks even through the shower spray, and I kissed them away before we both began to move.

This time was slower, taking our time where I hadn't thought we had it before. We could go hard and fast, go too much in the past, but right then, all that mattered was this moment with her.

And when she came again, I followed, filling her up to the point that my knees shook. I leaned against her, pressing her to the shower wall with my forehead on hers as both of us just let out a deep breath.

"Whoa," she said with a small laugh.

"That sounds about right," I teased. I kissed her softly again before I pulled out, and found a soft washcloth in the corner so I could clean us both up.

"Eventually, we're going to run out of hot water," she joked.

I snorted. "I built this house literally brick by brick,

and I know exactly how much hot water we have. Don't worry, I'll take care of you."

I kissed her again before we each finished showering and got out to get ready for the rest of the day.

We had woken up early so that we could have this moment to ourselves, and by the time we got downstairs, showered, fresh, and both laughing at something the other had said, the girls were just waking up and walking downstairs.

It had been three months since the fire; since we had nearly lost everything. And while I knew we would be okay, I also knew that it was going to take a little bit longer for the girls to truly believe that.

But when they both smiled at me, with Cameron ducking her face shyly and Alice running right to me, I couldn't help but feel as though I had finally found what I had been looking for since Amara had taken her last breath. Because I had done what she had asked, I had taken a chance at another forever, and I knew she was looking down at me, pleased and exasperated that I had finally done it. Because Amara would've loved this family.

And I was going to make sure the rest of the world knew that.

"So, are we really having an entire Wilder reunion today?" Cameron asked as she bit into her toast. I stood at the stove, finishing up the eggs and bacon, as Alice stood next to me, watching me work, and Rory finished cutting up the rest of the cantaloupe.

"Yes, there's going to be way too many of us, but don't worry, you're one of us now."

Cameron beamed. "I don't know, Cameron Wilder does sound like a good name."

Rory snorted and then looked down at the diamond ring on her finger, the one that I had given her only a week ago.

It might have been too soon for some, but with all we had gone through, neither one of us wanted to wait.

And after all, it had been Cameron and Alice who had helped me find the ring and make sure that the proposal worked exactly how we wanted it.

"You do not have to change your name if you don't want to," Rory said after a moment, worry in her gaze.

"I want to be Alice Wilder, and then we can keep Mommy and Daddy's name as a middle name like we promised." I met Rory's watery gaze and nodded solemnly.

"Don't worry, we'll make that happen. Do you want me to add another name to mine?" I asked out of the blue, and Cameron frowned.

"No, it's okay that we don't match completely. But I do like Wilder. It's a pretty name."

"I agree," Rory said. "Though Rory Wilder is kind of hard to say," she said dryly.

"I'm sure we can make it work," I added just as dry.

"And I get to be a flower girl with Faith, and Cameron gets to walk with Aunt Ava, and it's going to be a beautiful wedding."

"Of course it will be. The Wilders do good weddings. And good reunions. I guess we should finish up breakfast and head over there because there are way too many Wilders waiting on us at this point."

"And they're really going to help us move into your place?" Cameron asked, and I reached forward and messed with her hair. She scowled at me, straightening it again, and I couldn't help but snort. She was going to be a teenager any day now, and messing with her was just fun.

"Yes, my place is a little bigger, and you'll have enough space to move around and spread out. Is that okay with you?"

"We already said it was," Cameron said as she nudged Rory. Rory beamed up at me.

"Yes. And you let me pick out my own room."

"And this house will be just next door for whoever needs to rent it. And we'll make sure that it's a good family."

"And maybe they'll have kids to play with," Rory said with a smile.

"My friend Matt is looking for a new house," Cameron said shyly, and I narrowed my gaze.

"No boys. Sorry, that's just not going to happen. I know teenage boys."

"But Brooks," Cameron pouted, and I snorted before serving the rest of our breakfast.

"Nope, don't even think about it. You're stuck with me now, kid."

Cameron just beamed as if I had said the best thing in the world, and my heart grew two sizes at the thought. Because we were a family. Maybe not exactly how we could have been in other people's worlds, but we were exactly who we needed to be now.

THE WILDER RETREAT AND REUNION WAS JUST AS INSANE AS we knew it would be.

Thanks to the immense size of our family, we took up nearly every space with just family members and a few friends along the way.

Our innkeeper, Naomi, and her husband Amos, our vineyard manager, helped organize everything, and now stood on the dance floor, dancing with one another, with Amos's large hand on the small swell of Naomi's belly.

Jay and his husband, our wine specialists, were dancing next to them, both of them laughing about something the other had said.

Sandy, our sous chef and now partner with Kendall in one of the restaurants, danced with her wife, both of them trading places with Jay and his husband just for fun.

Each member of the team that had helped bring the Wilders to where they were was out there, no longer working, just enjoying their time with us.

And after such a long few years, it was nice to see them enjoying themselves. Mom and Dad sat at one of the head tables, all of their grandchildren around them. My cousin Eliza had come down from Colorado with her husband and a few of her in-laws, so the Montgomerys were in full force as well. Her two children, now older and in school, were laughing at something my mother had said, looked happy. Silas was now in preschool, while Lexington, the eldest of the next generation, held court over the others.

When Evan and Kendall's two kids, Reese and Cassie held the youngest ones with Kylie, Eli and Alexis's kid, helping the others out.

Not every one of my brothers and cousins had children, and I wasn't sure if all of them would, but everybody was making their next phases in life.

And as someone who thought that they were done growing and finding a future like this long ago, it was nice to see.

Eli and Alexis laughed in one of the corners, both of them whispering to one another, and from the way that Eli kept touching Alexis's belly, I had a feeling baby number three would be on the way soon. Kendall kept moving around to a thousand different places with the caterers, even though she shouldn't be working, and I laughed as Evan tugged her away, growling and threatening to lift her over his shoulder.

Everett and Bethany stood by the stage with East and Lark, the four of them sharing photos of some trip that they had just gone on for each one of the women's careers. The fact that Lark not only had the number one song in the world right now, but Bethany had the number one movie, just made me smile. It also made me laugh because Gabriel had the number two song in the world. So, of course, we had to make sure Lark lorded it over my brother.

Elijah and Maddie lay on the ground with their newest baby, both of them looking lost in the world and in each other's eyes as if they hadn't a care in the world.

While Sidney danced in my cousin Elliot's arms

before being twirled toward her other husband Trace's arms, the three of them a unit in a way that I hadn't even imagined possible when I had first moved here.

Aurora lay on Ridge's lap, his hand protectively over the swell of her belly, as they had just announced their pregnancy as well. After everything that my brother had gone through in the past, it was good to see him creating a family once again. And I knew Aurora, a widow just like I was, had found this second phase of her life difficult at first, and yet, she was thriving.

Wyatt and Ava ran around the room chasing Faith, who had a piece of cake she probably shouldn't have had, but as Aurora had been the one to make it, she just winked at the little girl and helped block her from her parents.

Everybody laughed, looking happy and excited to be there. And I watched as Rory gathered Cameron and Alice into her arms for a deep hug before going to sit over with my parents and listen to a story.

A familiar, tall shape sidled up next to me, and I looked over as Callum took a sip of his beer and frowned into it.

"Not up to your liking?" I asked the man who had slowly become my friend, even though it had taken a bit longer than it might have in other cases.

"Mine's better."

"We do have some of your beer here," I added dryly.

"True, but I like to taste the competition."

"And I guess there is no competition?"

Callum shrugged. "Not so much." He gestured towards his sister who stood laughing with Gabriel, and a now calmer Wyatt and Ava.

"She looks happy."

I nodded. "She is. I know they don't get to stay down here often because Gabriel's on tour, but we're taking care of her."

"So I hear. It's good that she has you guys down here and even the Montgomerys in Denver. She doesn't need to come up to Ashford Creek. It's better here."

I wanted to ask him why, to wonder why the lines between his brows kept deepening over time, but I didn't. This wasn't the time or place, and I didn't think Callum would tell me anyway. Instead, the other man took another sip of his beer, winced, and gestured toward another familiar face.

"Who's that?" he asked, pointing at the woman with newly bright red hair and a bright smile who pulled both Rory and Briar into her arms for a laughing hug.

"Kira. She's the drummer for Gabriel's band, remember?"

Callum nodded. "Oh, yeah. She looks different."

"New hair color, I think." I raised a brow. "Need me to introduce you?"

Callum just snorted. "What is it with happy people in relationships wanting to make everyone else happy in a relationship?"

"Honestly, this isn't the case. I had to deal with people setting me up for years after my first wife died. I'm not going to do that to you."

"And thanks for that, but no, I was just trying to remember where I saw her before. I remember now, though. She's not for me. Don't worry."

"You ever going to tell your sister or any of us who is?" I asked softly.

"There's nobody for me. But I'm fine with that. I'm going to head out soon, though as much as the Wilder reunion is welcoming, there's another reunion I need to attend soon."

I raised a brow, curious. "Everything okay there?"

"Not in the slightest, but don't worry, it won't fall back on the Wilders."

"That scares me, Callum. If you need anything, you call. You're not alone."

"Funny coming from you, the man who said he was better off being alone. But I'm glad you're not. Rory's a good person. Good for you."

"Don't make me get growly."

"No need to mark your territory. She's good for you. And not mine. And on that note, go kiss your future wife, and I'm going to say goodbye to my sister. Be safe, Wilder. You earned this." And with that, Callum walked off, and I frowned, wondering exactly what that particular Ashford had up his sleeve.

Rory came to my side then, wrapping her arms around my waist.

"Everything okay?"

I pushed her hair back from her face and nodded, a small smile playing on my lips.

"You're here. Everything's damn good."

"Now that's a line," she teased.

"I try. Do you want to dance, future Wilder?"

"So that's what you're going to go with?"

"Come on, let's go make out in the corner and annoy the girls."

"You are going to have fun with this whole guardian thing, aren't you?"

"Oh yeah. And we have plenty of people to show us the ropes so we don't mess up too badly."

"I love you, Wilder."

"I love you too, future Wilder. Thanks for taking a chance on me, even when I'm such a damn idiot. I almost lost it for both of us."

She cupped my face then and went on her tiptoes to

brush her lips along mine. I groaned into her, wanting to deepen the kiss, but I knew this wasn't the place.

"We might've both had our heads deep in the sand for too long, but now we're stuck with each other. And this very rambunctious family."

"Well, that's good to hear."

"Okay, pick up football game on the field. Nobody's allowed to back out," Eli called.

"That means I'm playing," Eliza said with a laugh, and Rory tugged on my arm.

"Come on, I love watching you play football."

"You just like to see me shirtless."

"I said what I said. But I get to play too."

"Anyone tackles you, I'm going to have to beat them."

"I trust you to take care of me," she teased, and as the girls ran to us and we made our way to the field, I held my family close, knowing that this wasn't the end, only the beginning.

And never something I could have ever wished for.

But something I would be grateful for till the end of time.

Because I was a Wilder, and so were the women in my arms.

And finally, finally, we could rest and look forward to whatever came next.

CHAPTER SEVENTEEN
CALLUM

It was easy to pack up your life when you didn't bring much with you. I had been gone from Ashford Creek for too long, and it was time to head back. Not only to the brewery but to the town that pretended they wanted nothing to do with me while clamoring for me to return.

My lip curled, thinking about what I needed to do as soon as I got home.

"Hey, you heading out?" a familiar voice asked and I turned to see Brooks standing in the doorway of my small room at the Wilder Inn, and I nodded tightly.

The man sure had leaned into his southern boy persona. Complete with boots, worn jeans, and a ball cap that he had taken off when he had come inside and tucked in his back pocket.

I wasn't sure if Brooks and I would ever be friends, but I liked the man. That was probably why I needled him as much as I did.

Hell, if I was honest, he reminded me of a little bit of Bodhi and a whole lot more of Rune.

I ran my hand over my chest, thinking about Rune. No, thinking about Rune and Atlas would only lead to me having a shitty trip home.

Especially when thinking about the two of them always led me to think about her.

Because my two best friends might be just as growly as Brooks sometimes was, but they wouldn't stop at kicking my ass for thinking about exactly what kept crossing my mind. And why I had even jokingly pursued Rory to begin with.

"I have work to do, plus I have to help my brother with some shit."

Brooks nodded. "That's always the way. So, do all of you Ashfords live up in your town now? It's a little weird that your name is the same as the town. Just saying."

I snorted at that. "It's not what you think. We're not the high and mighty Ashfords. One of our ancestors helped settle the town, and I'm pretty sure the lore is that they lost it on a drinking bet with shots, and that's why we got the name. But no, no one hears the mayor or some shit like that. The Ashfords aren't from the good side of our small town. Not that there's enough of town to have sides."

"Well, you may be an asshole, but I like Briar. So there's that."

I threw my head back and laughed. "Yeah, Briar is the good one of us. Well, and Teagan," I said, speaking of my other sister. "But Teagan is a lot like your sister-in-law, Ava. And can kick all our asses."

"That is the truth. She was nice when I met her."

"Yes, you're just meeting all the Ashfords now," said Brooks.

"I don't know... a few of you seem a little reclusive."

I snorted, because the guy didn't even know the half of it.

"Anyway, I'll be out of your hair soon. Thanks for putting up with me."

"Thanks for making sure I didn't have to kick your ass," Brooks teased.

"We both know it wouldn't have ended in your favor if you had tried," I said casually, doing my best not to look down at my hands.

My father's hands.

Even though I did my best to put a sense of teasing in my voice, I wasn't sure Brooks heard it. Instead, he gave me a nod and headed back to do whatever he was planning with this new life of his.

I liked Brooks. I hated the fact that he had lost his first wife. It was hell to lose someone close to you that you loved. I ran my hand over my chest. And the thing was, I wasn't even thinking about my brother. Malcolm had been gone for a couple of years now. Gone too soon, my baby brother.

No, there was the reason we were the way we were.

And it was about time that I figured out exactly what to do about it.

Because I wasn't going back to my small town just to get to work. And to pull Bodhi out of whatever the hell he was in now.

No, because I needed to find a woman. And not in a way that would make Brooks laugh. And not in a way that would make Brooks grin.

I needed to find a ghost.

Because if I didn't, then the truth we had all been ignoring for far too long would finally come to the surface.

Because Ashford Creek had its secrets.

Like the two women who'd disappeared from our family's lives.

The woman my dad might've killed.

And the woman I was pretty sure he did.

Our mother.

Thank you for loving the Wilder Brothers as much as I do!
Don't miss out on the next family saga, Ashford Creek! Callum Ashford finds his fate and his path in LEGACY.

IF YOU'D LIKE TO READ A BONUS SCENE:
CHECK OUT THIS SPECIAL EPILOGUE!

In the mood to read another family saga? Meet the Cage Family in The Forever Rule!

If you'd like to read the next Generation with the Montgomery Ink Legacy Series:
Bittersweet Promises

BONUS EPILOGUE

BROOKS

"**I** really wish she would take this blindfold off me," I grumbled. The hand on my arm tightened, tucking me toward wherever the hell they had planned for our evening.

"I bet that's not what you'd say to Rory," Gabriel teased. Even though I was still blindfolded, I was able to follow the sound of my brother's voice and punch him in the gut. The grunt that echoed helped this situation mildly.

"Seriously, where are we going? I don't like this."

"I am shocked. You don't like the unknown? No. Never," Ridge joked.

"I hate all of y'all."

"It's y'all," Wyatt corrected. "If you're going to be a true Texan, you have to realize there's a difference between all y'all and y'all."

"If I have to go through the singular versus plural versus angry possessive when it comes to the word y'all and any other colloquialism for stubborn-mindedness, for a fifth time, I will start punching again." I shook my head even as I said it, knowing the other guys were laughing their heads off as they led me to my fate.

"Okay, you bloody whiny baby. You can take your blindfold off," Gabriel added.

"You're not British either. Stop with that colloquialism."

"Just take off the fucking blindfold," Ridge spat.

"I truly love this feeling of togetherness. We, as a family, have really come together over the years. I can just feel the love, the caring, the closeness..." Wyatt trailed off as, thankfully, Gabriel punched him in the gut. I slid my blindfold off at the same time and shook my head at my three dumb ass brothers.

This wasn't exactly how I thought my life would be. Standing in a field wearing cowboy boots because it gave me better traction, warm jeans, surrounded by family, and what might be a rattlesnake. I narrowed my gaze at the stack of stones and shook my head.

"If you have taken me out to a field to bury me so I

have to somehow crawl my way back to Rory and emulate her favorite song, we're going to have a problem."

"I still can't believe her favorite song is from Hosier and not me," Gabriel said as he tsk-ed.

"Hey, it's the accent. You really can't help but love that Irish accent," Wyatt said as he fanned himself.

"Is there something we should know?" Ridge asked as he studied Wyatt.

My lips twitched, but I still studied the empty field.

"Where the hell are we?"

"We're right over that hill. This is your bachelor party." Wyatt held out his hands, and a drone firework burst in the sky.

I tilted my head, taking off my ball cap, and grinned.

"I guess we're getting around the fire ban?" I asked with a shake of my head.

"Really?"

"Hey, we spent weeks figuring out how to use this for events, so of course your party is our inaugural event." Elliot came over the hill and gestured for us to follow him. "And if we don't actually burn everything down, even though we don't have fire, it'll be at your wedding in two days."

A smile stretched over my face at that thought.

I was getting married. Again.

I wasn't quite sure how it had happened, but I was about to marry the second love of my life.

Because as Rory knew and held close to her heart, I would always love Amara. That was the funny thing about being human. Emotions and characteristics evolved. I was allowed to fall in love again, and I was damn lucky it was with a woman who saw me for who I was instead of the broken shambles of a man that she had met in the first place.

I hadn't expected Rory, and I knew she damn well hadn't expected me. But I was so fortunate.

Thinking about what-ifs and the idea that if Amara had lived, I wouldn't be with Rory didn't help anyone because there was no going back in time and finding a way to cure cancer and keep Amara out of pain. Leaning into those dreams only led me down the dark path and towards a bottle.

Instead, I was facing the truth and a future that Amara had paved for me.

I was going to marry one of my best friends. And I knew Amara would've fucking loved her.

I cleared my throat as I followed Elliot and my brothers over the hill to where the event planner himself had gone all out.

"Dear God," I mumbled as Gabriel laughed his head

off and joined the others as our eldest cousin, forty years old now, sat on a mechanical bull and was doing damn well at it.

"Apparently Eli did his twenty in the military and decided to lose his damn mind," Ridge mumbled.

"You're going to break a hip, old man," I called.

"Fuck you. I can still best you," Eli shouted, but he still only reached 10 seconds.

"I'm next," Everett said as he rubbed his hands together.

"I'm just running the damn thing. If I get on that, and Kendall hears about it, she's going to kick my ass. And we all know my wife can win any fight," Evan argued.

Elijah handed me a beer, and I just laughed as my cousins, friends, coworkers, and people who had joined our lives over the years celebrated my last day of bachelorhood. Although I wasn't quite sure if a widower was a bachelor. It wasn't as if there were flow charts and name tags for things like that.

I frowned at the beer in my hand. "I'm surprised you didn't give me wine."

"I figured you'd be in a beer mood. Plus, it's Callum's."

I lifted a lip in a snarl at the sound of Callum

Ashford's name. But as I looked over the lighted area where at least a couple dozen people milled about, I lifted my chin.

Callum lifted his right back as he continued his conversation with Trace.

"I'm going to like this beer, aren't I?" I grumbled.

"Yes, you will. And when the Wilders get into the beer business along with Roy, you're also going to like that beer."

Considering Roy had been the man who had gotten the Wilders into this whole line of work, I knew Elijah was right.

I took a swig of the beer, letting the light ale slide down my throat, then cursed.

"It's damn good."

"I hate him. So much," Elijah said, and I lifted my brows.

"Oh?"

"For you. I'll hate him for you. That's the Pilsner, and he has his IPA here too. He didn't bring the two yearly ones because they're for special occasions and out of stock."

"I brought a six-pack as a wedding present," Callum called as he pointed towards the cooler.

"It's three and three of our seasonals. Don't say I

never gave you anything other than Rory," Callum teased.

I handed my beer over to Elijah. "I'm going to go beat him."

"He's just fucking with you," Gabriel said with a laugh. "Plus, if you punch my brother-in-law, I don't know if I'm going to have to be on your side or on my wife's. It's a thing."

"I don't know how Briar deals with him."

"Her family can outrun us in drama. So give the man a break and just drink his beer," Gabriel said carefully, and I nodded and drank the damn amazing beer.

Beckett, our cousin-in-law, milled around, and I knew that his wife, Eliza, my cousin, was probably with the women for their bachelorette party.

Amos, the vineyard manager along with Finley, one of the guys in security, were up next on the bull.

I knew Finley had married some A-list actress, just like Everett had, and I couldn't help but wonder exactly how we had all changed so quickly.

East was now annoying Ridge about something, and Wyatt had forced Gabriel to bring out his guitar. And I leaned back in my seat, enjoying a bachelor party that was way more laid back than I had been thinking.

All that mattered was I was about to marry Rory. And the girls were going to be part of it.

A bona fide family, and exactly what Amara had wanted.

I tilted my empty beer bottle up at the sky, the stars blinking underneath the lack of light pollution.

"Love you, baby. And thank you for forcing me to listen. I'm just too damn hard-headed."

Another beer appeared in front of me, and as I took the seasonal one from Callum, he didn't say anything about my whispering to a ghost.

Instead, he tapped his bottle to mine, and I took a sip of the damn amazing beer that I knew was limited and made me hate him all the more.

The smile on his face told me he could read my thoughts, but I ignored him, and then after I finished the beer, I gave him the empty and started towards the bull.

"Okay, I guess it's time to show you the real wrangler here."

"You're not an actual cowboy," Gabriel called out.

"And your insurance won't let you on the damn bull," I teased.

"Because all of you guys tattle on me," Gabriel yelled back as people laughed.

I threw one leg up over the mechanical bull, settled myself, and hoped to hell I didn't end up with a black eye for my wedding.

I STARED INTO THE MIRROR AND PRESSED THE BLOSSOMING bruise on my jaw. It could be worse. Not much worse, considering what today was, but worse.

"Well, it's not a black eye."

I glared at Wyatt. "East and Evan must have made sure it was at the highest speed for me," I grumbled.

Ridge had the grace not to laugh. Instead, he turned away, even as I saw the humor in his gaze.

I had only made it seven seconds before I flew ass over tea kettle and somehow bruised my chin and elbow.

Rory, in her adorably drunken self thanks to the Wilder women and their wine, had kissed it better, and then I had kissed every inch of her skin just in case she had a bruise somewhere.

That had been two nights ago, and last night, I hadn't been able to see the bride.

Nor the girls.

Somehow, they had decided that the Wilders and their women all needed to be separate for the day.

Meaning every single cousin of mine was grumbly because they weren't with their women. But they would be tonight.

Thankfully.

"Are you ready for this?" Eli asked as he came forward.

I nodded, feeling far more relaxed than I thought possible.

"Yes. I've been ready."

Eli studied my face before nodding solemnly. "Yes, I think you are. Now, if I know my wife, she has her clipboard in hand and is ready to put us in our places. So let's make sure we're not late."

"Anything to make your wife happy," Wyatt joked.

I pushed past them, wanting to get to the ceremony as quickly as possible.

Because then I would see Rory.

"There you are, baby boy," Mom said as I turned and hugged her tightly.

"I'm just heading to the altar. You ready for this?" I asked.

"My babies have all flown the coop and are making babies of their own. I'm so ready for this." She patted my cheek and narrowed her gaze at the bruise. "Boys. Wild. All of you."

"We're your kids. I'm not quite sure why you're surprised."

"I guess I'm not. By the way, you did a good thing,

inviting Amara's parents," she whispered as people milled about, heading towards their seats.

I swallowed the lump in my throat and nodded.

"They sent a gift, and Rory was the one that reached out. However, I know it would've been too hard for them to be here."

"But they sent their blessing. And I know Amara is here with us all."

"Don't make me cry before I see my bride. She's already going to get grumbly about the bruise."

"I thought she already saw it?" she asked as I led her to her seat next to Dad.

"Yes, but I don't think she thought about wedding photos."

"Well, it'll be a story. The girls will remember it, and any future babies will remember it," she teased.

"Mom. One thing at a time," I said with a laugh.

I kissed her cheek, hugged Dad, and went to stand up next to Wyatt, my best man.

"Places, everyone," Alexis said, and I met Eli's gaze while holding back a laugh.

Yes, Alexis Wilder, wedding planner extraordinaire, kept us on our toes and exactly where we needed to be.

The music began, and I swallowed the lump in my throat as Alice walked down the aisle, small bouquet in hand. We had offered for her to be the flower girl, but she had said she wanted to be an attendant. So, instead of flower girls and ring bearers, we decided just for the girls, Ava and Rory, to be part of the ceremony. We could do things on our own terms.

Alice wore an adorable champagne-colored dress that made her strawberry-blonde hair stand out and look radiant. And as she waved to me, I winked back at her.

People laughed, and then Cameron was walking down the aisle, looking like a young adult and scaring the hell out of me.

She was a teenager now, with bright eyes and a lifted chin. And she was going to be my daughter. Yes, I would always be Uncle Brooks to her, but in all ways that mattered, she was mine. Just like little Alice, and just like the woman walking behind Ava.

Cameron and Alice took their places at the front seats next to Briar and the others while Ava stood across from me, winking at her husband. But I had all eyes for Rory.

She was stunning in a mermaid gown of lace and silk that I knew reminded her of one of the heroines she had drawn for a book she loved.

It even had a flowing cape instead of a veil or train, and she looked like the queen she was.

I didn't even realize I was walking towards her until Wyatt laughed, and the others joined in.

But I held out my hand halfway down the aisle and smiled.

"Hello there," I whispered.

"Impatient?" she asked as her hand went up to the bruise on my chin.

"Always."

And as a breeze settled through her hair and down over her hand and to my bruise, I knew exactly who that was. And who had also given their blessing.

And from the look in Rory's gaze, she knew too.

Because I loved this woman. With everything that I had in me.

I was going to marry her and call her mine, and I was way too damn impatient. We walked hand in hand up to where the officiant stood, and I let out a deep breath.

I had made a promise, a promise I knew I would fail at keeping. But in the end, it was a promise kept and a forever that I knew would never end.

Because life sometimes gave you second chances, as long as you understood the first chance paved the way for fate to have its say.

And Rory was mine. Endlessly and forever.

Thank you for loving the Wilder Brothers as much as I do!

Don't miss out on the next family saga, Ashford Creek! Callum Ashford finds his fate and his path in LEGACY.

A NOTE FROM CARRIE ANN RYAN

Thank you so much for reading **Endlessly Yours.**

The Wilder Brothers are somehow coming to a close...but you never know. I could always return! But don't worry, until then, we're headed to Ashford Creek and a brand new family saga with LEGACY!

The Wilder Brothers Series:

Book 1: One Way Back to Me (Eli & Alexis)

Book 2: Always the One for Me (Evan & Kendall)

Book 3: The Path to You (Everett & Bethany)

Book 4: Coming Home for Us (Elijah & Maddie)

Book 5: Stay Here With Me (East & Lark)

Book 6: Finding the Road to Us (Elliot, Trace, and Sidney)

Book 7: Moments for You (Ridge & Aurora)

Book 7.5: A Wilder Wedding (Amos & Naomi)

Book 8: Forever For Us (Wyatt & Ava)

Book 9: Pieces of Me (Gabriel & Briar)

Book 10: Endlessly Yours (Brooks & Rory)

Thank you for loving the Wilder Brothers as much as I do!

Don't miss out on the next family saga, Ashford Creek! Callum Ashford finds his fate and his path in LEGACY.

IF YOU'D LIKE TO READ A BONUS SCENE:
CHECK OUT THIS SPECIAL EPILOGUE!

If you want to make sure you know what's coming next from me, you can sign up for my newsletter at www. CarrieAnnRyan.com; follow me on twitter at @CarrieAnnRyan, or like my Facebook page. I also have a Facebook Fan Club where we have trivia, chats, and other goodies. You guys are the reason I get to do what I do and I thank you.

Make sure you're signed up for my MAILING LIST so you can know when the next releases are available as well as find giveaways and FREE READS.

Happy Reading!

ACKNOWLEDGMENTS

Spending time with the Wilders have truly changed my life. I'd had this idea in the back of my mind for years, but I had to be ready for it. It was always a personal series for me because of the way it came about. I'm a military kid, surrounded by veterans. Many get out of the military and find themselves lost. They'd had full time jobs as engineers, managers, and more, and suddenly didn't fit into the world the same again.

I wanted to write a series where brothers came back and looked out for each other. And in the current world, we *have* to look after each other. And that's what the Wilders did.

This final book was about hope and loss. Broken promises. And taking that next leap. As a widow myself, I understood Brooks's path like no other. Because our hearts can find ways to open up for another chance at love when fate takes our first chance away.

And I'm forever grateful to to be able to write them.

So thank you, Dear Reader, for allowing me to go

along this journey and make the Wilders a part of my family.

Thank you to Team Carrie Ann for your help on this one. We wrote it in parts over time because of well... *waves hand around* *everything*. I'm so glad we finally got it off the ground and were able to get this book in the readers' hands.

Thank you to my family for listening to me as I tried to work my way through Rory's path. It wasn't easy and I'm so grateful to you for not turning me away when things got hard!

Thank you for everything, Wilders. I'll miss you. But then again...I'm terrible at goodbyes. So maybe it's not goodbye forever...

~Carrie Ann

ALSO FROM CARRIE ANN RYAN

The Montgomery Ink Legacy Series:

Book 1: Bittersweet Promises (Leif & Brooke)

Book 2: At First Meet (Nick & Lake)

Book 2.5: Happily Ever Never (May & Leo)

Book 3: Longtime Crush (Sebastian & Raven)

Book 4: Best Friend Temptation (Noah, Ford, and Greer)

Book 4.5: Happily Ever Maybe (Jennifer & Gus)

Book 5: Last First Kiss (Daisy & Hugh)

Book 6: His Second Chance (Kane & Phoebe)

Book 7: One Night with You (Kingston & Claire)

Book 8: Accidentally Forever (Crew & Aria)

Book 9: Last Chance Seduction (Lexington & Mercy)

Book 10: Kiss Me Forever (???? & ????)

The Cage Family

Book 1: The Forever Rule (Aston & Blakely)

Book 2: An Unexpected Everything (Isabella & Weston)

Book 3: If You Were Mine (Dorian & Harper)

Book 4: One Quick Obsession (???? & ???)

Ashford Creek

Book 1: Legacy (Callum & Felicity)

Book 2: Crossroads (??? & ???)

Clover Lake

Book 1: Always a Fake Bridesmaid (Livvy & Ewan)

Book 2: Accidental Runaway Groom (??? & ???)

The Wilder Brothers Series:

Book 1: One Way Back to Me (Eli & Alexis)

Book 2: Always the One for Me (Evan & Kendall)

Book 3: The Path to You (Everett & Bethany)

Book 4: Coming Home for Us (Elijah & Maddie)

Book 5: Stay Here With Me (East & Lark)

Book 6: Finding the Road to Us (Elliot, Trace, and Sidney)

Book 7: Moments for You (Ridge & Aurora)

Book 7.5: A Wilder Wedding (Amos & Naomi)

Book 8: Forever For Us (Wyatt & Ava)

Book 9: Pieces of Me (Gabriel & Briar)

Book 10: Endlessly Yours (Brooks & Rory)

The First Time Series:

Book 1: Good Time Boyfriend (Heath & Devney)

Book 2: Last Minute Fiancé (Luca & Addison)

Book 3: Second Chance Husband (August & Paisley)

Montgomery Ink Denver:

Book 0.5: Ink Inspired (Shep & Shea)

Book 0.6: Ink Reunited (Sassy, Rare, and Ian)

Book 1: Delicate Ink (Austin & Sierra)

Book 1.5: Forever Ink (Callie & Morgan)

Book 2: Tempting Boundaries (Decker and Miranda)

Book 3: Harder than Words (Meghan & Luc)

Book 3.5: Finally Found You (Mason & Presley)

Book 4: Written in Ink (Griffin & Autumn)

Book 4.5: Hidden Ink (Hailey & Sloane)

Book 5: Ink Enduring (Maya, Jake, and Border)

Book 6: Ink Exposed (Alex & Tabby)

Book 6.5: Adoring Ink (Holly & Brody)

Book 6.6: Love, Honor, & Ink (Arianna & Harper)

Book 7: Inked Expressions (Storm & Everly)

Book 7.3: Dropout (Grayson & Kate)

Book 7.5: Executive Ink (Jax & Ashlynn)

Book 8: <u>Inked Memories</u> (Wes & Jillian)

Book 8.5: <u>Inked Nights</u> (Derek & Olivia)

Book 8.7: <u>Second Chance Ink</u> (Brandon & Lauren)

Book 8.5: Montgomery Midnight Kisses (Alex & Tabby Bonus(

Bonus: Inked Kingdom (Stone & Sarina)

Montgomery Ink: Colorado Springs

Book 1: Fallen Ink (Adrienne & Mace)

Book 2: Restless Ink (Thea & Dimitri)

Book 2.5: Ashes to Ink (Abby & Ryan)

Book 3: Jagged Ink (Roxie & Carter)

Book 3.5: Ink by Numbers (Landon & Kaylee)

The Montgomery Ink: Boulder Series:

Book 1: Wrapped in Ink (Liam & Arden)

Book 2: Sated in Ink (Ethan, Lincoln, and Holland)

Book 3: Embraced in Ink (Bristol & Marcus)

Book 3: Moments in Ink (Zia & Meredith)

Book 4: Seduced in Ink (Aaron & Madison)

Book 4.5: Captured in Ink (Julia, Ronin, & Kincaid)

Book 4.7: Inked Fantasy (Secret ??)

Book 4.8: A Very Montgomery Christmas (The Entire Boulder Family)

The Montgomery Ink: Fort Collins Series:

Book 1: Inked Persuasion (Jacob & Annabelle)

Book 2: Inked Obsession (Beckett & Eliza)

Book 3: Inked Devotion (Benjamin & Brenna)

Book 3.5: Nothing But Ink (Clay & Riggs)

Book 4: Inked Craving (Lee & Paige)

Book 5: Inked Temptation (Archer & Killian)

The Promise Me Series:

Book 1: Forever Only Once (Cross & Hazel)

Book 2: From That Moment (Prior & Paris)

Book 3: Far From Destined (Macon & Dakota)

Book 4: From Our First (Nate & Myra)

The Whiskey and Lies Series:

Book 1: Whiskey Secrets (Dare & Kenzie)

Book 2: Whiskey Reveals (Fox & Melody)

Book 3: Whiskey Undone (Loch & Ainsley)

The Gallagher Brothers Series:

Book 1: Love Restored (Graham & Blake)

Book 2: Passion Restored (Owen & Liz)

Book 3: Hope Restored (Murphy & Tessa)

The Less Than Series:

Book 1: Breathless With Her (Devin & Erin)

Book 2: Reckless With You (Tucker & Amelia)

Book 3: Shameless With Him (Caleb & Zoey)

The Fractured Connections Series:
Book 1: Breaking Without You (Cameron & Violet)
Book 2: Shouldn't Have You (Brendon & Harmony)
Book 3: Falling With You (Aiden & Sienna)
Book 4: Taken With You (Beckham & Meadow)

The On My Own Series:
Book 0.5: My First Glance
Book 1: My One Night (Dillon & Elise)
Book 2: My Rebound (Pacey & Mackenzie)
Book 3: My Next Play (Miles & Nessa)
Book 4: My Bad Decisions (Tanner & Natalie)

The Ravenwood Coven Series:
Book 1: Dawn Unearthed
Book 2: Dusk Unveiled
Book 3: Evernight Unleashed

The Aspen Pack Series:
Book 1: Etched in Honor
Book 2: Hunted in Darkness
Book 3: Mated in Chaos
Book 4: Harbored in Silence
Book 5: Marked in Flames

The Talon Pack:

Book 1: Tattered Loyalties

Book 2: An Alpha's Choice

Book 3: Mated in Mist

Book 4: Wolf Betrayed

Book 5: Fractured Silence

Book 6: Destiny Disgraced

Book 7: Eternal Mourning

Book 8: Strength Enduring

Book 9: Forever Broken

Book 10: Mated in Darkness

Book 11: Fated in Winter

Redwood Pack Series:

Book 0.5: An Alpha's Path

Book 1: A Taste for a Mate

Book 2: Trinity Bound

Book 2.5: A Night Away

Book 3: Enforcer's Redemption

Book 3.5: Blurred Expectations

Book 3.7: Forgiveness

Book 4: Shattered Emotions

Book 5: Hidden Destiny

Book 5.5: A Beta's Haven

Book 6: Fighting Fate

Book 6.5: Loving the Omega

Book 6.7: <u>The Hunted Heart</u>

Book 7: <u>Wicked Wolf</u>

The Elements of Five Series:

Book 1: From Breath and Ruin

Book 2: From Flame and Ash

Book 3: From Spirit and Binding

Book 4: From Shadow and Silence

Dante's Circle Series:

Book 1: <u>Dust of My Wings</u>

Book 2: <u>Her Warriors' Three Wishes</u>

Book 3: <u>An Unlucky Moon</u>

Book 3.5: <u>His Choice</u>

Book 4: <u>Tangled Innocence</u>

Book 5: <u>Fierce Enchantment</u>

Book 6: <u>An Immortal's Song</u>

Book 7: <u>Prowled Darkness</u>

Book 8: Dante's Circle Reborn

Holiday, Montana Series:

Book 1: <u>Charmed Spirits</u>

Book 2: <u>Santa's Executive</u>

Book 3: <u>Finding Abigail</u>

Book 4: <u>Her Lucky Love</u>

Book 5: Dreams of Ivory

The Branded Pack Series:

(Written with Alexandra Ivy)

Book 1: <u>Stolen and Forgiven</u>

Book 2: <u>Abandoned and Unseen</u>

Book 3: <u>Buried and Shadowed</u>

ABOUT THE AUTHOR

Carrie Ann Ryan is the New York Times and USA Today bestselling author of contemporary, paranormal, and young adult romance. Her works include the Montgomery Ink, Redwood Pack, Fractured Connections, and Elements of Five series, which have sold over 3.0 million books worldwide. She started writing while in graduate school for her advanced degree in chemistry and hasn't stopped since. Carrie Ann has written over seventy-five novels and novellas with more in the works. When she's not losing herself in her emotional and action-packed worlds, she's reading as much as she can while wrangling her clowder of cats who have more followers than she does.

www.CarrieAnnRyan.com